Corpse AND **ROBBERS**

A MALE HOUSEKEEPER MYSTERY

BY

STEPHEN KAMINSKI

Copyright © 2022 by Stephen Kaminski

For information, visit our website at:
www.cozycatpress.com

COZY CAT
PRESS

ISBN: 978-1-952579-45-5

Printed in the United States of America

10 9 8 7 6 5 4 3 2 1

For Kristin

Floor Plan
of
Paul Bearer & Sons
Funeral Home
Rusted Bonnet, MI

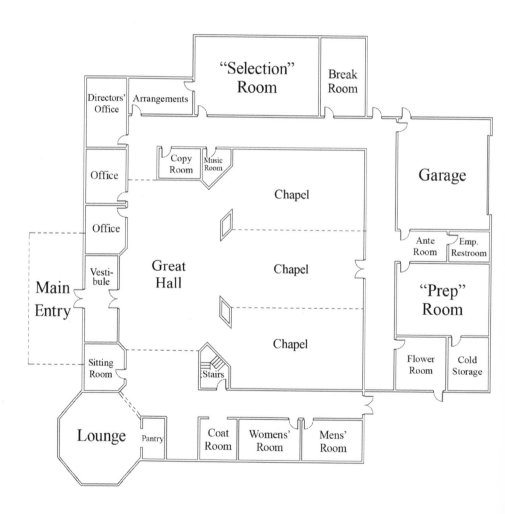

"Selection" Room

Break Room

Directors' Office

Arrangements

Copy Room

Music Room

Office

Garage

Chapel

Office

Chapel

Ante Room

Emp. Restroom

Vesti-bule

Great Hall

Chapel

"Prep" Room

Main Entry

Chapel

Sitting Room

Stairs

Flower Room

Cold Storage

Lounge

Pantry

Coat Room

Womens' Room

Mens' Room

Chapter 1

Sunday, February 7

"Free figs?"

"Free figs yesterday, Braeburns last Saturday, and fennel the week before that," Cam Reddick said, elbows resting on his kitchen countertop.

A teapot wheezed in staccato gasps.

"I'll get it." Kacey Gingerfield plucked the kettle from the stovetop. She poured hot water into three caramel-colored ceramic mugs, then added tea bags to two and a splash of cold milk, instant cocoa mix, and mini-marshmallows to the third. "Emma, your hot chocolate's ready," Kacey called out. To Cam, she whispered, "Free produce three weeks in a row? That doesn't sound like a mistake."

"My thoughts exactly," Cam replied, accepting a mug from Kacey. His ex-wife's thick, dark hair rippled around her ears. She'd stopped by his townhouse to pick up their newly-minted seven-year-old daughter.

Emma rushed into the room, a blur of blond locks bobbing

around her ears. She retrieved the mug of cocoa from Kacey's outstretched hand and walked with painstaking precision back in the direction of Cam's living room.

"Ten more minutes, Emma!" Kacey called after her. "You have school in the morning."

Cam glanced up at the neon green numbers on the microwave oven—7:30 p.m.—then back at Kacey. She had hoisted herself onto a stool, and was sitting cross-legged, drinking from her mug.

"How's the chamomile?" he asked.

"Perfect for a night like tonight." The temperature had dipped into the low teens—Mother Nature rarely joked during the heart of winter in Rusted Bonnet, which lay in the southern half of Michigan's well-known thumb.

"No kidding." Cam warmed his hands around his mug.

"So free fruits and veggies. Do you think the cashiers are surreptitiously slipping food to all of the customers? Maybe trying to put the store owner out of business?" Kacey served as Deputy Chief of the village police department.

Cam held up a hand. "I don't think it's anything like that." He sipped his tea, then added a drizzle of honey from a plastic bear waiting patiently on the laminate countertop. "I've shopped at the grocery here almost every weekend since moving back and have a pretty good rapport with most of the staff. Store clerks, stock boys, managers." Cam leaned forward. "Usually, I go to whichever check-out line a guy named Ramón is working. We get along really well—he's about my age."

"You've been in Ramón's line each of your past three trips to the store?"

Cam nodded. "Here's the rub. For Christmas, I gave a few of the folks there a card with a small cash gift inside. Just those who I see all of the time—a thank you for their good service.

No different than the mailman."

"Or Emma's bus driver," Kacey said. "That's very kind of you."

Cam shrugged. "I didn't think it was a big deal. The Saturday morning shift manager told me he thought it was a nice gesture. Well, I gave Ramón more than the others. I know he's supporting his sister and baby niece and that can't be easy. It wasn't anything too extravagant—a hundred dollars instead of a ten." He touched his tongue to the rim of his mug where a drop of honey had beaded. Deliciously sweet. "I doubt any of the other employees knew I'd given Ramón that much—it was inside a card in a sealed envelope. He probably didn't even open it until he got home."

"And ever since, he's been repaying your generosity with fennel and figs."

"Apples, too. The first couple of weeks after New Year's, I didn't see him at check-out. I think he took some time off after the holiday rush. Two weeks ago, I didn't even realize he skipped ringing up the fennel until I checked my bill at home. It never occurred to me that it was anything other than a mistake, even though he's a careful checker. Last week, I happened to scan the receipt before leaving the store. I saw that he didn't charge me for the Braeburns—I almost went back and said something, but didn't want to get him in trouble. It could've been a coincidence. For all I knew, he was working a night shift somewhere to pay the bills and his check-out skills were slipping from exhaustion."

"But you were suspicious?"

Cam nodded. "Yesterday, I spaced out my groceries on the conveyor, more so than usual, and watched him closely."

"And he purposefully overlooked the figs?"

"It certainly looked that way. I had four fresh ones in a plastic produce bag. Ramón set the figs in front of him as if to weigh them, then asked me who I was rooting for in the Super Bowl. While I answered, he grabbed a prepackaged bag of spinach leaves from the belt, scanned it and then swept them both into my grocery bag. But he never punched in the ID code for the figs, so they didn't get charged. I was too shocked to say anything." Cam smiled, then added, "Don't arrest me, okay?"

Kacey grinned, showing the smallest hint of an overbite. "I wouldn't think of it. Fennel, apples, and figs—all produce. Do you think there's a reason for that?"

"I imagine it's harder for the store to track. I don't know what kind of inventory they do, but I bet a few missing apples wouldn't be noticed as easily as cans of soup. Not that I think Ramón is passing free produce to anyone but me. I watched him check-out the customer in front of me and the one behind me, too."

"Did you hang back and pretend to tie your shoe?" Kacey smirked.

"Actually, I pulled out my phone and had a fake conversation with you." Cam snorted. "I didn't see him make any 'mistakes' on anyone else's purchases."

"So, if he's not out to bilk the store, what's his angle?"

"At first, I figured he wanted to make sure I gave him another big gift next Christmas, but I'm not sure that's it." Cam paused. He twisted his neck and peered past the dining room into the living room. Emma was multi-tasking: crafting a multi-thread bracelet with an open book in her lap and a Disney Jr. cartoon blazing across the LCD. Cam refocused his attention on Kacey. Small, gold, hoop earrings dangled from her teardrop-shaped earlobes. "I'm just shooting from the cuff, but I think he's trying to say thank you."

"Shooting from the cuff—is that your latest malaphor?"

"You know me—you can't teach a junkyard dog new tricks." Cam smiled. "I think Ramon is repaying me in the only way he can. I have a feeling he was raised not to accept anything without returning the favor."

"I suppose, but you'd think with such an upbringing, stealing would be a no-no, too." Kacey stretched, raising her arms above her head. Cam admired her. Since moving back to Rusted Bonnet from a Washington, D.C. suburb almost a year earlier, he'd not only reconciled with her, but was making a concerted effort to regain her trust and establish a connection with Emma. They had even gone out on a "date," but afterward, Kacey told him she wasn't ready for more than a friendship, at least for the time being.

"I guess passing along the produce is the lesser of two evils. For all I know, he slips a few extra bills into the till from his own pocket to pay for my 'free' groceries."

"So, what are you going to do?" Kacey asked. Her chocolate brown eyes were fixed on his blues.

"I'm not sure. I can't let it continue. But I don't want to say anything to his manager, either. He'd probably feel obligated to take a-action." Cam's voice caught. "I probably shouldn't have told you."

Kacey laughed. "Because I'm a police officer? Don't worry, Cam, I'm not going to bring Ramón in for filching some figs."

"I suppose I have to confront him. Tell Ramón that I don't need free produce."

"You don't have to be so direct. Save him the embarrassment."

"So, what do you recommend?" Cam sipped his tea.

"That's the million-dollar question."

***

Monday, February 8

Samir Orucov and his wife, Mitzy, operated Paul Bearer & Sons Funeral Home. Not that Mitzy did much other than drink champagne cocktails and lord over the aging home and its staff like a blitzed baroness. Christened "Leyla," Mitzy was the daughter of a peasant farm worker and housewife in Azerbaijan. She was swept off her feet at the age of eighteen by the dashing young Samir, who whisked her to America with a devilish smile and the promise of opportunities abound. After short stints in Cape May—a beach town in New Jersey—and Wichita, the couple landed in Rusted Bonnet. Samir started out sweeping floors at Paul Bearer's, worked his way up to the top spot— funeral director—and by the time old man Bearer retired, had saved enough money to slap down a down payment and take ownership of the non-denominational home. There were, in fact, no "sons" to assume the business.

Samir, a fifty-three-year-old Azerbaijani from Baku had grown up in a world very different from Mitzy's bucolic childhood. From the age of eight, he slept on city streets with his older brother, Jalil, surviving off of poached farmer's market fare. By twelve, Samir realized that Jalil—then sixteen and with more brawn than wits—didn't have the chops to get them out of their cardboard box quarters behind a printer's shop. So, Samir assumed the role of the brains behind the pair of brothers, and devised a set of confidence schemes. Within a year, he had them living in a rented room at the back of a brothel, and by the time he turned twenty, Samir and Jalil shared a penthouse on the coast overlooking the azure blue waters of the Caspian Sea.

But Samir fancied himself as a businessman rather than a con artist, and had an itch to see America. His plans to travel overseas were slowed when he spotted Leyla—then a fetching teen selling produce and fending off lecherous men behind her father's stall in a downtown market. He took the time to court her properly, wooing her with rich silk dresses and expensive dinners. Within a year, they married and—over her father's protests—hopped on a plane to the United States. Samir left

Jalil behind, armed with stacks of cash and a working knowledge of enough simple ruses to get by on his own.

Samir quickly learned that life as an immigrant was no picnic in the States. Nor was making a living aboveboard. After failing ventures in the wholesale carpet and kitchen cabinetry trades, he reverted to the deception profession. But New Jersey law enforcement didn't accept dollars the way Baku policemen greedily shoved banknotes into their pockets. So, the couple fled Cape May for Kansas, where Leyla tried her hand at hawking costume jewelry and Samir at peddling bags of livestock feed laden with healthy doses of sawdust. Neither was successful and after Samir spent twelve months in Leavenworth, the pair tucked their tails between their legs and moved to Rusted Bonnet, where Leyla had a second cousin working as an electrician at the local Ford engine plant.

Suppressing his dreams of a corner office in a skyscraper, but not giving up on America, Samir accepted a minimum wage position with Paul Bearer & Sons. At the same time, Leyla took a fancy to Bellinis and to Bacardi chased with pineapple juice, dubbed herself Mitzy and, a year later, bore a son.

Cam learned the entire history of the Orucov family from Mitzy, who nominally held the position of funeral attendant. Despite pushing into her late forties, Mitzy's willowy figure and deft hand with a makeup kit clawed ten years back when she looked in the mirror. And she never failed to show off her figure —usually by donning tight-fitting yoga pants and strappy tank tops—any time he cleaned the funeral home.

Cam manned the helm of Peachy Kleen, the housekeeping service his mother Darby had started in her twenties. As soon as he set foot back in Rusted Bonnet eleven months earlier—after five years floundering in dead-end jobs and coming to terms with the mistakes he'd made as a young man—Darby handed him the keys to the company.

Business was sound at Peachy Kleen. Four full time cleaners —two older women who'd been with Darby for years and a mother-daughter team of African descent—made up the crew. Cam spent a majority of his time soliciting new clients, balancing the books, and keeping supplies at the ready, but managed to tackle a handful of properties, too—his least favorite part of the job. Unlike Peachy Kleen's residential clientele where Cam sent staff in pairs, Samir requested that a single housekeeper scrub down the funeral home every two weeks—to preserve an air of calmness should a potential client pass through. And Cam had to admit, that he enjoyed working by himself with nothing but an ancient iPod and his thoughts to keep him company. But because cleaning the funeral home took close to eight full hours, he and one of his seasoned housekeepers—Tabby Vasquez—took turns.

By four o'clock on Monday afternoon, Cam was halfway through the Paul Bearer job. An emergency trip to Sears for a new steam mop to replace one that had died on Becka Blom— the daughter in Peachy Kleen's mother-daughter pair—set him off to a late start. He'd finished the two largest areas of the home: the "Great Hall" and the enormous chapel with its walls of peeling seafoam-colored paint. But collectively, the home's smaller spaces—the offices, lounges, and restrooms—took just as long to detail. Not to mention having to face his two least favorite areas: the "Selection" room filled with caskets on offer and the "Prep" room for embalming.

"Your carpet in the chapel is starting to fray," Cam said to Mitzy as she entered the "Flower" room where he was dusting. The small space toward the rear of the building had an exterior door, presumably to allow for deliveries without disturbing front of the house activities.

"I know," Mitzy huffed in exaggerated exasperation. "Samir has become cheap." A tight-fitting plum-colored sweater and black stretch pants hugged her curves. As Cam bent over to wipe down a maple tabletop, Mitzy set down a tumbler filled with an inch of yellowish-brown liquid, brushing her body against the back of his leg. She straightened up and said, "When I met Samir, he was all flash. Condo on the sea, fancy watch, he even smelled like money. Now?" She waved a hand in the air. "*This* is my seaside chalet. Stuck in the sticks with a flabby, greasy husband and an idiot son. No excitement."

"Maybe you and Samir should go on a vacation," Cam suggested, taking a step away from Mitzy. "Somewhere exotic."

"Two weeks in Turks and Caicos with the fat man? I don't think so." She paused, then added, "Of course, drinking piña coladas with my toes in the sand without Shane or that lunkhead friend of his would not be so bad."

Before Cam could respond, the exterior door swung open and two young men plodded inside, carrying heaps of earth in their arms. Wearing stained flannel shirts and dirty jeans, they looked to Cam like a pair of pig farmers. Loose soil and gravel trickled from their holds, leaving a trail on the rubber floor.

"What the hell, Shane?" Mitzy shouted. "Mr. Cam here is *cleaning*. Get that dirt out of here!"

"Sorry, Mom," the thinner of the men said. "We got a request to fill planters for the Szubek viewing. Dad told us to get potting soil."

Cam snickered despite himself.

"Potting soil comes in bags, you dolt," Mitzy said.

"So, what should we do with this?" the other man asked.

Before Mitzy could respond, Shane dumped his load on the center of the table. His counterpart followed course. A reddish-pink worm pushed though the top of the pile.

"It was getting heavy," Shane explained. "Mom, we dug up all of this good ground. Should we take it back or use it for the planters?"

Mitzy clapped a hand against her forehead, picked up her drink, and downed the rest of the liquid. "Where did it come from?"

"Under one of the cherry trees outside."

"In plain view of the parking lot?" Mitzy exclaimed. "Someone will think we're digging graves right here!"

Shane stubbed a muddy boot against the floor. "We'll put it back."

"Do not pick it back up in your arms," Mitzy demanded. She looked at the larger of the men. "Go see if you can find something to put that dirt into. There should be a wheelbarrow in the shed out back."

"Yes, Miz Orucov, there is," Heath 'Jelly Roll' Sands replied. "The shovels were inside it."

Chapter 2

Shane Orucov had never been diagnosed with an intellectual disability; he was just slow. *Chances were good,* Cam thought, *that his condition correlated to Mitzy drinking heavily during pregnancy.*

"No viewings, today?" Cam asked him after Mitzy had excused herself to refresh her beverage. Cam sprayed Windex on the flower room's front window.

"None today," Shane said. He leaned against the earth-covered table. "We have two tomorrow. Dad asked us to pitch in to get ready for old man Szubek's funeral." Cam knew that Shane primarily served Paul Bearer's as a courier—picking up death certificates from the hospitals and delivering them to the county registrar. Shane's friend and roommate, Jelly Roll, piloted a hearse for a living, but both took on bits of manual labor for the home as well.

"Did you know him?" Cam asked to make conversation. "Szubek, I mean."

"The old man? No. But I played hockey with his grandson.

Hot shot, Chet was. Got hisself a full ride to some school out east. Suppose he'll be here tomorrow." Shane scrunched up his face, his upper lip touching the tip of his nose. Only in his mid-twenties, his hair was already graying. With mutton chop sideburns and a protruding forehead, he reminded Cam of a prematurely aging werewolf—more Mr. Hyde than Michael J. Fox.

A moment later, heavy boots thudded against the door. Shane opened it to Jelly Roll who maneuvered a Fanta orange wheelbarrow into the flower room and parked it alongside the table. The heavyset man wiped his brow with the front tails of his shirt, then handed a shovel to Shane.

"I suggest you set that down," Cam said to Shane. "You wouldn't want to scrape the maple."

"True. Sure is a nice table."

"Everything in this place is mighty nice," Jelly Roll remarked. "Your ol' man must be swimmin' in dough."

Like Mitzy, Cam didn't think the home was well kept, but remained silent. Samir was a regular client and those were the lifeblood of Peachy Kleen.

"He could pay us more, that's for sure," Shane said and started to sweep dirt with his hands into the wheelbarrow. "If this place were mine, I sure wouldn't live in the apartment upstairs like Mom and Pop do."

"But it would be nice to get outta' our rat's nest," Jelly Roll said and started to push dirt with his pink, meaty paws.

"We could get one of those lofts in Royal Oak. Over the nightclubs. Live large. Bring back the ladies every night."

"Every night for sure wit' a place like that."

***

Markuss Vitolins and Blair Lamb looked as mismatched a pair as Shane and Jelly Roll were similar. Markuss was an aging embalmer and Blair, a Macy's makeup counter girl who moonlighted as a mortuary cosmetologist. Two cadavers were laid out face-up on treatment tables in front of them—Markuss's on an embalming table and Blair's on a corpse cart. White cabinetry, a sink, and an assortment of tubes connected to a tabletop embalming pump adorned the white tiled "Prep" room under powerful UV lights. Vats of unidentified pink and clear liquids and a panoply of instruments—scalpel, medical scissors, and a menacing piece of spiked metal fashioned into a hook—stood ready on the countertop.

When Cam entered, rags and detergent in hand, Blair looked up. A dust mask covered her nose and mouth, highlighting sand-colored eyes under her bell-shaped eyebrows. Blair's older sister had been named Homecoming Queen when Cam was a high school senior. The following year, local pageant organizers pressed Blair, four years her sister's junior and in an unworldly class of natural beauty, to compete at the state level. "To start."

According to Samantha Krause, one of Cam's mature cleaning ladies whose nose for gossip could leave a competing bloodhound on the dole, Blair was disgusted by the idea. She had no intention of allowing hordes of "busybody women" and "creepy old men" to ogle her body. But Blair's mother, with visions of escorting her daughter to New York and Cannes in flowing gowns, pushed her.

Blair revolted. Not with cigarettes and cheap beer or by covering her body with ink, but by cramming as many calories into her tiny body as she could muster. Her mother crafted sack lunches of grilled chicken breasts and apple slices. Blair tossed them in the trash as soon as she hit the school's front door, opting for lard-laden French fries from the cafeteria. After leafy green dinners at home, she snuck off to Taco Bell and Pizza Hut. And during study sessions, drama club, and babysitting gigs, downed Little Debbie's finest. According to Samantha, it worked like a charm. Not only did her cheeks begin to bloat but her skin turned into an oil slick that bested Proactiv's most zealous salvo.

Once Blair turned eighteen, she changed course and entered cosmetology school. Not that she cared about her looks, at least according to Samantha, but because she feared eating herself into an early grave. Now, at twenty-nine, Cam thought she was the finest looking woman in the village. According to Samantha, she had dated a couple of men and at least one woman.

"Looks like you guys are busy, why don't I come back later," Cam said to Blair.

She smiled at him with her eyes. Through the dust mask, presumably worn to ward off the smell of formaldehyde that permeated the air, she said, "I don't know about Markuss, but I'll be finished in just a minute. Mrs. Alabaster here was an easy job. She never flinched a bit." Blair pulled down her mask and grinned. Cam couldn't be sure whether Alabaster was indeed the elderly woman's last name or if Blair was poking fun at the stony face, lightly softened by her rouge brush. An enormous ruby resting in the hollow of the deceased woman's neck contrasted sharply with her brown tweed suit and sensible shoes.

"I'm almost done as well," Markuss Vitolins said in a gruff voice that mirrored his cobblestone complexion. He wore a navy-blue surgical gown. In his mid- or late-sixties, Markuss served as Rusted Bonnet's embalming staff of one, splitting time between the village's two funeral homes.

Cam studied the top of Markuss's head as he wielded a needle and suture thread. Liver spots spread across his naked crown like chocolate chips in a melting cookie.

"Is that Mr. Szubek?" Cam asked.

"It is." Markuss looked up at Cam. "Who are you, one of

Shane's friends?"

"Markuss, this is Cam," Blair cut in. "He's one of the cleaners. You've met him before."

Markuss grunted and bent his head back down, finishing his task. "So long as you're here," he said after a minute, "you might as well make yourself useful and help me get this lump off of the slab."

Markuss wheeled in a cart from an anteroom and parallel parked it next to the embalming table. On Markuss's "go," the two men rolled Mr. Szubek from his back on the embalming table onto his stomach on the cart.

"Miss Lamb," Markuss wheezed, "You're touching up the body before the viewing tomorrow, correct?"

"I am," Blair said. "His show starts at three. Missus mole-on-her-cheek here goes on at ten."

Markuss crooked a finger and Cam taxied the dead man's cart into an adjacent storage room, which was bare save for a double-decker, stainless-steel mortuary cooler—he'd heard Shane call it the "corpse fridge."

Markuss followed. "Help me slide him in," he said and punched a code into the keypad on the cooler. Markuss cracked opened the top hatch and pulled out a retractable steel bed, noticeably wincing. "Darn arthritis," he said, guiding the dead man's head and shoulders onto one end of the bed.

Cam hoisted the feet—they were Yukon cold to his touch. "I didn't realize a freezer was needed after you embalm a body," he said. They twisted the body onto its back.

A gray tooth marred Markuss's smile. "Good observation. You're definitely not one of Shane's friends. Technically, once the body's embalmed it's no longer needed, but we have to store the body somewhere and most funeral directors don't like to keep them out where a visitor could accidentally stumble by."

Markuss glided the bed with the deceased octogenarian into

the top drawer of the cooler, knocked the door shut with an elbow, and set the lock. He stripped off surgical gloves and his face mask. "That's that. Done for the day." He looked at Cam. "I'll leave you to clean up. I have to get the missus off to water aerobics." Shaking his head, he added, "Crazy woman. Doesn't she realize it's the dead of winter and a storm's supposed to hit tonight?"

***

A brass handrail in the octagonal-shaped lounge at the front of Paul Bearer's shimmered from a heavy dose of Brasso and the pressure of Cam's forearms. He was wiping polish from his fingertips when Samir tramped down the stairs from his living quarters, a roast beef submarine in one hand, a can of Faygo Rock & Rye in the other.

Patterned ripples of gray streaked Samir's neatly-trimmed beard like an M.C. Escher print. Broad shoulders stretched a horizontal-striped sweater that looked as if it had danced with the washing machine one too many times.

"You're still here?" Samir asked from the entrance to the lounge.

"I got off to a late start. I probably need another hour or so down here." Cam regarded his watch. It was nearly six o'clock and darkness was closing in fast. "The snow's starting to come down pretty hard," he said glancing at heavy flakes pummeling a southwest-facing window.

"There must be a wind, too," Samir observed.

"Do you mind if I come back in the morning to clean the apartment?"

Samir sipped his soda. "That's a good idea. You should get home before the roads get too bad. Just as long as you can get in and out tomorrow before the ten o'clock service."

"Absolutely," Cam said.

"Good." Samir wrinkled his brow. "There might be a bit of a mess up there in the morning. Mitzy's already tanked and trashing the walk-in."

"The closet?"

"Apparently her clothes aren't good enough anymore. She's piling up anything without a label from Milan or Paris." Samir laughed, the lids of his hooded eyes bouncing. "Are you married, Cam?"

"Divorced," he replied quietly.

"Good man. Marriage is a wonderful institution, but who wants to live in an institution?"

***

Apparently, Darby Reddick wasn't in the mood to pull punches. "Did you even notice the snow outside?" she barked.

"I just drove through it," Cam said, setting a sack of groceries on her front hall table. He stripped off his Duck boots on the braided rug at the foot of the stairs, then shed a wool driving coat.

After finishing at the funeral home, Cam had stopped by the market to pick up staples for his mother, but purposefully avoided Ramon's line. Since retiring, Darby lived in the world of fixed income and despite her protests, Cam continued to make small contributions. He considered them nominal payments for Peachy Kleen, which she'd turned over to him, asking for no more than a peck on the cheek. A stable of steady clients and the established goodwill were worth tens of thousands of dollars, if not six figures.

And Cam knew that Rusted Bonnet was a better place for a housekeeping company than many of the surrounding communities. It mirrored thousands of small Midwestern towns with family-owned shops sharing sidewalk space with closed storefronts. But unlike most of its kin, mature automotive facilities circled the village, salvaging its economy with humdrum but steady shots of green insulin. The pockets of relative affluence supported a smattering of eclectic boutiques, an upscale hair salon, and a chocolatier.

"The weatherman said we're looking at anywhere from four to six inches overnight," Cam said. "There'll be plenty of drifting with that wind out there, too."

"All the more reason you should be at home. But since you're here, how about some hot soup? You can sleep in your old room tonight if you'd like."

"Thanks," Cam said. He picked up the groceries and strode into the kitchen, exchanging the bag with his mother for a steaming mug of split pea. "I was over at Paul Bearer's. The store and your place are on my way home."

"Likely story," Darby said with a smile. She set the bag on the hardwood floor and slid gracefully into a chair at the kitchen table, twisting her graying blond hair around a pencil and into a bun. "How are Samir and Mitzy?"

"All right, I suppose," Cam said, then recalling Samir's comment about divorce, added, "though I'm not sure they're getting along perfectly."

"I don't know of many married couples who do. Your father and I, God rest his soul, had our share of tiffs. Is Mitzy still drinking like a fish? I swear that woman had a cocktail in hand every time I cleaned the place."

"Samir told me she was three sheets flapping in the wind. That was before six o'clock." Cam tasted the soup—thick with potatoes, just the way he liked it. He knew firsthand how difficult marriage could be, especially if one of the two "life" partners lacked the will to compromise. In his case, he knew that person had been him.

Shortly after college, Cam and Kacey—high school sweethearts—had married. Unlike her, he wasn't ready for children and she knew it. So, when the little blue plus sign reared its head, Kacey cowered in a corner of their bedroom closet rather than leaping into his outstretched arms. Cam validated her fears by distancing himself emotionally and making a litany of poor decisions. In time, he lost his job as well as his wife and baby daughter. Since his return to Rusted Bonnet, Cam had discovered a tenacity he never realized was lurking inside and harnessed it into the resolve he needed to become a good man and a good father. He had even helped Kacey solve a murder the previous fall—the first in the village for as long as anyone could remember.

"Do you know Samir and Mitzy well?" Cam asked, cupping his hands around his soup mug to warm them.

"Well enough, I suppose," Darby said, tucking a bare foot under her backside. "They've been Peachy Kleen clients for more than ten years. You get to know folks if they're around when you're working, of course."

"True."

"Mitzy doesn't hide her vice. Samir's another story. He can be a charmer when he puts his mind to it."

Cam looked up at his mother. "Did he hit on you?"

Darby laughed. "Just about every time I set foot in the place."

"Really?" Cam arched his eyebrows.

"Surprised? Shame on you, Cam."

Shame on him for not realizing Samir was a ladies' man or for underestimating his mother? "You swatted him away?" he asked.

"Of course. Besides being married, the man's a rascal."

"A rascal?" Cam mocked.

"He was in prison."

"Mitzy told me. The whole con artist history. She's a bit flirtatious with me, you know."

"Mitzy?" Darby smiled. Her teeth were immaculately white. "No surprise there. You know, a few years ago, one of Samir's funeral attendants was arrested."

"Really?"

"Apparently, he swindled some older folks out of their social security checks. I don't recall the details, but something Samir said at the time stuck with me."

Cam cocked his head to the side.

"He told me that people tend to hire their 'own type.' I remember because I think he's right to some degree. I see a lot of my own traits in the Peachy Kleen staff I hired." She sipped her soup, then added, "But it made me wonder how many other crooks were on the payroll at Paul Bearer's."

Chapter 3

Tuesday, February 9

Two's company, three's a crowd.

The acrid stench of death greeted Cam when he arrived to clean the Orucov's apartment. Paul Bearer's had two funerals on the schedule, but three dead bodies.

Moments earlier, Cam had pulled "Virginia"—one of Peachy Kleen's three vans—into the funeral home's spacious snow-covered parking lot. He'd noticed two police cruisers parked alongside Samir's dated Lincoln, Mitzy's Cherokee, and a third vehicle.

Cam stomped his boots on the outside mat and entered the great hall, wheeling a cleaning cart. An early weekday morning should have been calm in the hall with its low-lit yellow table lamps, propane-fueled fireplace, and taupe-colored sofas: Samir and Piper Quick—Paul Bearer's other funeral attendant who, unlike Mitzy, actually put in a hard day's work—briskly but quietly arranging chairs, music, and programs for the ten o'clock viewing. Mrs. Never-Did-Catch-Her-Name. But today was a different story. Samir and Piper were indeed in the hall, along with Mitzy, Kacey, and the Chief of Police, Bernie Leftwich. Only, one of them wasn't breathing.

Samir Orucov lay flat on his stomach in the cut-out between the great hall and the center third of the trifurcated chapel, the hilt of a knife unceremoniously protruding from his back.

To the left of the body, Piper leaned against the frame of the entry. The fortyish-year-old redhead's close-cropped hair hugged her scalp. She jabbed tissues at her eyes, smearing mascara down elfin cheeks.

On the opposite side, Mitzy stood like a sentry in a teal shift and boy shorts, showing a solid eight inches of toned thighs. Flip flops shunned an exterior wind chill in the low teens. She showed no sign of the prior night's inebriation, but Cam couldn't interpret her expression. His best guess—smugness laced with expectancy.

As Cam approached, his cart thumping over the carpet, Kacey, who was hunched over Samir's body on the chapel side, looked up. "Cam," she said sharply. "Stop right there. Can't you see this is a crime scene?"

Cam pulled back on the two push handles of the cart, halting its momentum.

"What are you doing here?" Bernie Leftwich barked.

Cam inched around the cleaning cart, closer to Samir's body. Rivulets of red snaked like a starburst down the back of Samir's blue-and-white pinstriped oxford. The carpet on either side of his body appeared stiff with dried blood. "We clean every two weeks. I wasn't able to finish last night because of the storm. Samir told me to come back first thing in the morning to do the apartment."

"You were here last night?" Bernie asked, narrowing his eyes at Cam. "And you saw Samir?"

"Of course."

"What time was that?"

"About six o'clock, in the lounge. I just had one more office and the music room left down here. I wanted to head out before the snow got too deep."

"What time did you leave?"

"Just before seven."

"Did anyone see you go?"

Cam twisted his head toward Kacey. She averted her eyes. A light clicked on in Cam's head. "Are you suggesting that I stabbed Samir?"

"Should I be?" Bernie snarled.

"Of course not!" Cam shouted. He leaned back against his cart. It started to roll and he stumbled onto his backside. *Ouch.*

"Was anyone else here when you left?" Bernie asked.

"Not that I know of." Cam jumped up and stopped the cart. "I didn't see any of the staff and I'm pretty sure Samir had gone back upstairs. He said Mitzy was tearing apart the bedroom closet."

Mitzy looked down at her flip flops.

Kacey asked her, "Were you?"

"I'm reorganizing," she mumbled.

Chief Leftwich said, "I don't care about a bunch of women's clothes. It sounds to me like no one saw you leave. There sure are a lot of places to lie in wait around here."

"Stop accusing me! I was at my mother's house last night."

"Your mother's house?" Bernie scoffed. "Not much help there. I don't know a mother who wouldn't cover for her son."

Cam shook his head vigorously. "I brought her groceries," he said. "You can check my credit card—I picked up milk and bread and eggs at Alwards."

"Darby fancied French toast?" Mitzy said with a smirk.

"What?" Cam shot back. "No. I bought other things, too."

"How could someone do th-th-this?" Piper wailed. She took

a step toward Samir and dropped to her knees. "He never hurt anyone."

Mitzy muffled a laugh.

Piper shot her a look of contempt. She opened her mouth, then snapped it shut.

"All right, everyone," Chief Leftwich said. "This whole funeral home is a crime scene. Both floors." He looked at Kacey. "Deputy Gingerfield, cordon off the perimeter of the property—the parking lot and the yard on the sides and back of the building, too. Wrap the tape around stakes in case it starts snowing again. We need people kept out of here."

"But we have two memorial services today," Piper protested.

Bernie shook his head slowly, the blue veins in his cheeks flaring. "I don't think so. I'd recommend you call the funeral parlor over on Monroe and see if they can take a couple of extra wakes or viewings or whatever they're called. Once we've scoured this place, I'll let Miz Orucov release the bodies." He started to chuckle, then checked himself. "Not Samir's, of course."

"The place on Monroe is *Catholic*," Piper said in a hushed voice.

Bernie shrugged. "Do what you want, but no one's setting foot in here for the rest of the day. Probably longer." He looked at Mitzy. "I need you to clear out of the upstairs. Can you stay with your son?"

Mitzy threw the chief a glare drenched in disgust. "You are kicking me out of my own home? No way I am staying in Shane's dump with that Jelly Roll boy." She breathed in dramatically. "I will find a hotel."

"Good," the chief replied. To Piper, he said, "What time did you arrive this morning, Ms. Quick?"

"About ten after seven. I unlocked the front door, shucked my boots and coat in the vestibule, and saw poor Samir. I called

9-1-1 straight away."

"Good," the chief said and laid a hand on Piper's shoulder. "You should go now. Someone will come by your place for a formal statement this afternoon. Miz Orucov can call you when I give the go ahead for this place to re-open."

He removed his hand and turned to Cam. "As for you," Bernie said. "We need to talk sooner rather than later." The chief looked at Kacey. "Deputy, put Mr. Reddick in one of the offices here to wait while we look around. And don't let him touch anything."

***

"Does Chief Leftwich really think *I* could have killed Samir?" Cam whispered to Kacey as they made their way with Piper through the great hall toward a small suite of offices near the front of the funeral home. Bernie and Mitzy were headed in the opposite direction.

Kacey stopped near the front door. "I'll be in touch soon," she said to Piper as the redhead slipped into knee-high rubber boots and a parka.

Piper nodded and pushed her way outside. A pulse of cold shot in before Cam yanked the door shut.

Kacey said, "I doubt he seriously suspects you. More likely, he's still upset that you solved Greta Astor's murder last fall. He didn't appreciate the picture the *Observer* painted—you as the brilliant amateur detective and him as the appreciative fool. I think he just sees a chance to take out his frustration on you."

"Well, that's just peachy-dory. I hope he doesn't keep up the charade for too long. He let Piper go. If she arrived before anyone else, how is she less suspicious than me? Plus, I gave him a perfectly good explanation of what I was doing last night. One that he can verify."

Kacey hummed noncommittally.

"What?" Cam asked.

"You know I have no doubt as to your innocence, but a credit card receipt and eyewitness accounts from a grocery clerk and your mother don't amount to a rock solid alibi."

"For heaven's sake, why not?"

"You said you saw Samir at about six o'clock in the lounge, correct?"

Cam nodded and scuffed a shoe against the carpet.

"I understand that Mitzy was upstairs at the time. And no one else was here, right?"

"I'm pretty sure Shane and Jelly Roll left. The embalmer said he had to take his wife to water aerobics. And I hadn't seen the cosmetologist for some time."

"Do you see the problem?" Kacey placed a hand on his forearm. "You didn't leave until seven. Theoretically, that gave you an entire hour to kill Samir, quickly finish scrubbing the rest of the downstairs here, then pop into the grocery store and over to your mother's house. Which, by the way, seems a bit illogical if the reason you didn't clean the apartment was because you wanted to get home before the storm got too bad."

"I spent the night at my mother's!" Cam shouted. He ripped his arm away from Kacey's hand. "Whose side are you on?"

"Yours," she insisted. "But I'm just looking at it from Bernie's point of view."

"Anyone could've come in and killed Samir after I took off. The front door wasn't locked when I left."

"Piper said she unlocked it this morning."

"Meaning Samir or Mitzy locked it," Cam said through gritted teeth. "Or *Piper* could be lying."

"Possibly. Or the killer locked it on his way out."

"You'd need a key to bolt it from outside."

"There's no deadbolt." Kacey pointed at the front door's jamb.

Cam grunted.

"Sorry. I'm just doing my job here, Cam."

Cam took a deep breath. "I know. I've just never been accused of murder before."

Kacey smiled meekly. "You'll be fine. Do you know where Samir went after you spoke with him in the lounge?"

Cam pushed his thumbs against his earlobes. "He told me he was going to the selection room—a shipment of new caskets came in yesterday and he said he needed to unwrap them."

Kacey shuddered.

"I bet he never imagined he'd end up in one of them," Cam said, then quickly added, "Sorry, that was tasteless."

Kacey turned toward the office suite. "Come on, I have to park you and then brave the cold and get cracking with the police tape."

"Hold on," Cam said. "Won't forensics be able to tell what time Samir died? If it's any time after I bought groceries, I should be in the clear."

"They'll give us a range, which will certainly help." She stepped down the narrow corridor leading to the funeral home's offices, walked to the corner, and screamed.

Chapter 4

Cam rushed to Kacey's side. Markuss Vitolins lay face up in the hallway in front of the music room. Splotches of red stained the carpet to his right.

"Call the paramedics!" Cam shouted at Kacey, then cried, "Help!" as loudly as he could.

As Kacey punched numbers into a smart phone, Cam dropped to his knees and put an ear against Markuss's chest. He could feel it shallowly expanding and contracting. Markuss's eyes were closed, but a small sound like a baby bird's cry wheezed from his lips. "Hang in there," Cam whispered.

"Get away from him!" Chief Leftwich roared as he tore down the opposite side of the corridor. Mitzy trailed him.

"Is he alive?" Bernie bellowed and stopped at Markuss's feet.

"He's breathing," Cam said, rising and stepping backward.

Kacey hung up her phone. "The paramedics are on their way."

Bernie squatted down to look at Markuss. "There's blood underneath him," he said. "It's probably a stab wound, too."

"But no knife," Kacey observed.

"The killer probably stabbed this guy first, yanked out the knife then rammed it into 'ol Samir. What's this man's name?" Bernie twisted his head to look at Mitzy.

"Markuss. He is the embalmer here. Do you *officers* not inspect everywhere when you come? My husband is lying dead and you do not find Markuss here? If he dies, it is on *your—* what is the word?—conscience!" She planted her hands on her hips. "On the television, the first thing the police do is '*secure the scene.*' Is a murderer in my home? Ready still to pounce!"

Kacey looked down at her feet.

Bernie blustered, "For Pete's sake, we were trying to establish the circumstances around your husband's death. No killer in his right mind would stick around waiting for the police to arrive."

"So you say," Mitzy said. "But you do not know."

Kacey knelt next to Markuss and squeezed his palm, as if trying to pump blood back into his body. Cam could see the edge of a tear in the back of his shirt.

"But just to be sure," Bernie said, "Deputy, why don't you check the rest of the home while we wait for the paramedics."

Kacey rose to her feet and strode off briskly. Cam lowered himself and took over the pumping of Markuss's hand, not that it seemed to be having any effect on the man. But his breathing hadn't ceased. *Was he in a coma?*

"I'll call his wife," Mitzy said. "My phone is upstairs."

"Stay where you are," Bernie commanded.

"*Now* you are concerned?" Mitzy mocked.

Cam handed Mitzy his mobile phone.

"I do not know the number," she said. "May I look it up on the white pages?"

Cam agreed. Bernie paced as Mitzy pecked at the phone with manicured nails, then put it to her ear.

"Should we flip him over and take a look?" Cam whispered to Bernie.

"Hell, I don't know," he said.

Mitzy finished her call and handed the phone back to Cam. "She is coming directly."

Seconds later, someone screeched, "Paramedics!"

"Here!" Bernie shouted back. He skirted Markuss and disappeared around the corner in the direction of the entry. Ten seconds later, Bernie returned, trailed by a strapping young man with circular eyes and a sharp nose—a dove's face—and an older woman. Her rolled-up sleeves showed off forearms the size of overgrown yams.

"Step back, please," the woman said to Cam and Mitzy with a tone of authority.

Bernie clamped a hand on Cam's elbow. "Come with me," he said and started to lead him away from Markuss in the direction of the office suite.

"Don't you want to see his wound?" Cam pleaded.

"I can do that at the hospital," Bernie said gruffly. "No need for *you* to see it." He shepherded Cam into a small room tucked in between Samir's corner office and the home's "front" secretarial space. "Don't leave this office," he said. "I'll be back later to interview you properly." The chief confiscated his phone —so he didn't get any 'clever ideas about calling his mother to tell her his alibi.' Then Bernie slammed the door shut behind him.

***

Twenty green oblong pills. Cam stared down at a pair of foil blister packs. He flipped one over and read "1 mg. Flunitrazepam," stenciled in blue on the back of each serrated square.

After sitting for an hour in the office, staring at cheaply framed prints of French bistros with captions lauding the influence of early *plein air* impressionists on the artist, Cam had started to poke around out of boredom.

Bricks of Post-it notes and flimsy boxes of binder clips and staples filled the overhead cabinets. Blue and white banker's boxes stacked four high lined the walls. Cam lifted the lid of one—it divulged nothing but pages of records inside: copies of death certificates, receipts for casket purchases and sales, invoices for "mortuary services." The second box he opened contained handfuls of programs, memorial prayer cards, and thank you notes. Standard funeral home fare, he figured.

Rummaging through the desk drawers yielded more old papers—most dated five or more years earlier. But at the back of the bottom drawer, under a pile of tax forms, he unearthed a stiff cardboard box with pretty pink and white stripes—a pricy parcel the size of a tissue box. Natural curiosity prompted him to lift the lid. To his disgust, his eyes met a cheap plastic tray of melted moldy chocolates: a broken and congealed cherry cordial, green-speckled toffee, a truffle sprouting truffles—a sampler of Whitman's nightmares. Cam's first thought was to toss the box in the trash, but instead, propelled by instinct, he lifted a corner of the tray with the point of a pencil. His eyes widened at the sight. Cam quickly shot a look at the door—still closed.

He pinched the corner of the russet-colored plastic and gingerly pulled it away to reveal a yellow packing envelope snugly tucked underneath, one corner stamped with a New Delhi postmark. Cam unfolded the bubble-lined mailer, reached inside, and pulled out the packets of green pills.

Flunitrazepam. He didn't recognize the name and had no means of identifying the pill. Cam cursed Chief Leftwich for commandeering his smart phone and Samir for keeping an office barren of a computer or landline to call Poison Help.

Thirty minutes later, Kacey entered without knocking. "Ready for a few questions?" she asked.

"I'd be thrilled to do anything other than sit here," Cam said. "The chief's letting you interview me?"

"It's not ideal, but Markuss regained consciousness so Bernie went to the hospital. And he doesn't trust any of the junior officers to work a murder."

"If Markuss spotted his attacker, his golden goose will be cooked."

"I have my fingers crossed."

"Then for my sake, I sure hope Markuss saw the guy. Is there any chance we can talk somewhere else? I've been in here for an hour and a half."

Kacey led Cam toward the break room. As they passed the selection room, she said, "Mitzy told me Shane and his buddies used to play hide-and-go-seek in there when he was a teenager. They'd crawl into the caskets and everything."

Cam shook his head. "That's disturbing. Then again, I can't imagine growing up above a funeral home."

Kacey shut the door to the break room. A drab, olive green couch fronted a low wooden table littered with fashion and motorcycle magazines. Five folding chairs circled a plastic table next to a kitchenette, complete with cooktop, sink, and microwave.

Kacey sat in a folding chair. Cam stayed on his feet. "I've been sitting forever," he explained then removed a blister pack from his back pocket. He tossed the pills on the table. "Do you have any idea what these are? I found them hidden in one of the office's desk drawers."

"Hidden?" Kacey repeated as she reached for the tablets.

"I was bored," Cam said with a shrug. He described the box of moldy chocolates while Kacey inspected the packet. She yanked a smart phone from her pants pocket and jabbed at the screen. A minute later, she said, "These are roofies!"

"The date rape drug?"

"You got it. Flunitrazepam's the generic name for Rohypnol."

"The mailer had a postmark from India."

"I'm not surprised," Kacey said. "You can buy almost any pharmaceutical from overseas without a prescription. Not that it's legal. Do you have any idea who they belong to?"

Cam shook his head. "The address on the envelope was blacked out with marker. There were two packets inside. I put the other one back in the drawer where I found them."

"You can show me when we're done here. Thanks, Cam. I'll check our database to see if we have any open date rape cases."

"Is there any chance there's a medical use for the pills?" Cam asked. "Something legitimate for the preparation of a dead body?"

Kacey crinkled her nose. It was dotted by faint brown freckles. "I suppose anything's possible. Of course, we can't ask Samir. Maybe I can run it by Markuss if he recovers." She rubbed her eyes. "Then again, if someone had a lawful reason to possess Rohypnol, why hide the pills?"

"Good point," Cam conceded.

Kacey stuffed the packet and her smart phone into her handbag on the floor near her feet. "Now, let's walk through everything that you did between arriving here yesterday afternoon and returning this morning."

Chapter 5

"So, you didn't see anyone come in before you left at seven o'clock last night?" Kacey asked when Cam finished his narrative.

"No." Cam scratched his chin. "But, I had the vacuum running part of the time. And there are quite a few doors to this place."

Kacey sipped water from a plastic cup. "Six to the outside, not counting the garage."

"Were they all locked?" Cam asked.

"The door to the flower room and the one next to this room weren't. Mitzy said they aren't religious about securing the place at night."

"I'm not surprised. Why would anyone break into a funeral home? There doesn't seem to be much to steal."

"Au contraire." Kacey smiled. "There's plenty in here to tempt a burglar. And I'm not even counting the fact that the Orucovs have an apartment upstairs."

"Like what?" Cam asked. "A casket?"

"For one, yes. Do you have any idea how expensive those are?"

"A few hundred dollars?"

"More like a few thousand," Kacey said. "But I was referring to jewelry."

Cam frowned. "Why would a funeral home have jewelry?"

"On the *bodies*," Kacey said. "Mitzy said tons of women get buried with their wedding rings on. Men with their favorite watch. Things like that."

"Has Paul Bearer's ever been robbed?"

"According to Mitzy, only once. Last night."

Cam raked his fingers through his short brown hair, then pressed them against his temples. "Old Mr. Szubek or the woman? Mrs. Ten a.m. Service."

"More like Mrs. Missing-Her-Ruby-Necklace," Kacey said. Abruptly, she stood. "I can't believe I just said that. Or told you any of this. You're a suspect, Cam."

"Kacey," Cam said, imploring her with his eyes. "Please sit. You know I have nothing to do with any of this. Wasn't I a help the last time you had a murder on your hands?"

Kacey remained standing, but clamped her hands over the back of her chair. "Of course, you were. But the chief didn't exactly appreciate your assistance."

"I know," Cam said quietly, then perked up. "Wasn't her body locked in the cooler?"

Kacey stared at him. "How did you know that?"

"I helped Markuss heave the other body, Mr. Szubek, into the upper deck of it yesterday. Blair was finishing up on the woman —I figure she probably loaded her body into the lower compartment when she finished."

Kacey winced, the reason unclear to Cam.

"Was Szubek robbed, too?" he asked. "I don't remember him wearing a watch or anything. I did see that big ruby the woman was wearing."

"According to Mitzy," she said, "nothing was taken from

Mr. Szubek. But she recalled admiring the ruby when the woman came into the home two days ago. And, of course, they catalogue all personal effects. She showed me the ledger—Mrs. Hazel Bitter. A three-carat ruby on a 24-karat-gold chain. Trillion cut." Kacey stared at him.

Cam sensed that Kacey was testing him, but couldn't interpret her face. His only thought was that the dead woman had a name—Mrs. Bitter. "I'd be bitter too if someone snatched my three-carat necklace," he said with an exaggerated smirk.

Kacey cracked a weak smile.

"Do you think this was a robbery gone bad?" Cam asked. "Someone sneaks in through an open door, swipes Mrs. Bitter's necklace, then runs into Samir and Markuss as he's trying to get away."

"Maybe," Kacey said noncommittally. She rubbed her hands together. "I've already said too much. You're free to go, just make sure you don't leave town."

"Don't leave town?" Cam juddered. "What did I miss? Two minutes ago, you were acting normally. All of a sudden I'm a *real* suspect in your book, too?"

Kacey's eyes softened. "No," she said gently. "I trust you. I wouldn't have let you back into Emma's life if I didn't. I just have to be careful is all." She turned and walked toward the door.

As she twisted the handle, Cam said, "Hold on." His mind was churning. "This must have been an inside job, right? If Hazel Bitter was locked in the cooler, whoever took the necklace had to know the combination. So, it must have been someone on Paul Bearer's payroll."

"Either that or someone who saw an employee open the cooler—like someone who was helping load a body inside."

***

Kacey's words stung, though he knew she was right. Cam hadn't been paying attention to the numbers Markuss punched into the mortuary cooler when they slid Mr. Szubek's body inside, but he could have.

That explained Kacey's change in demeanor—the realization that Cam could have accessed Mrs. Bitter's body.

"So, *I'm* a suspect," Cam said with irritation.

Bait stared at him intently. The rescue fish finished his evening meal while Cam paced back and forth in front of the octagonal tank in his dining room.

Cam pulled a hard-backed chair away from the lacquered table and sat facing Bait.

"If a robber broke into the funeral home to steal Mrs. Bitter's necklace from the cooler, why was Samir killed between the great hall and the chapel? Check that; 'broke in' is too strong. If the killer was an employee, he'd probably know that Samir and Mitzy weren't vigilant about locking up at night. Maybe Samir saw the robber and ran. He was chased down and stabbed."

Bait whipped off three quick circles around the tank. "You're right, that doesn't make sense," Cam said. "Markuss was attacked, too. I think the robber got to Markuss first, yanked out the knife, then did in Samir." He paused. "Or I suppose there could have been two knives. Chase and kill Samir first, then use a second knife on Markuss, and take that one with him. Of course, for all I know, there could've been two robbers."

He cracked his knuckles. Bait shot him an annoyed look. "Sorry, force of habit," Cam said. He stood and recommenced pacing. "What do we know for sure? Unless Blair forgot to lock it, the killer knew the combination to the mortuary cooler. Who would know that?"

Cam ticked the names off on his fingers. "Other than Samir and Markuss, there's Mitzy, Shane, Piper, and Blair, even though she's not full-time. Jelly Roll might know it, too. That makes five."

Cam stepped into the adjoining kitchen. He opened the refrigerator and rooted round inside. "Seven," he said loudly after a minute. "Discounting Samir and Markuss might be a mistake. One of them could have been the inside man." He snapped his fingers. "He teams up with another thief and waits until there's a body with a valuable piece of jewelry. Like that huge ruby. He calls in the outsider after everyone leaves for the night and they open the cooler. Maybe the other guy is the fence and they planned to split the proceeds. Only, once the cooler's unlocked, the fence has other ideas—he wants the whole score to himself and stabs his partner. But to his surprise, he's seen. So, the fence has to stab another man—Markuss if the crook is Samir, or Samir if the crook is Markuss."

Cam smiled with self-satisfaction. He pulled out Tupperware containers of leftover tomato soup and gluten-free egg noodles, dumped the contents into an earthenware bowl, and let the microwave work its magic. "Who's more likely to be the bad guy here, Bait?" he asked, wandering back into the dining room as the soup reheated.

"Samir's a jailbird. Maybe old habits die hard. But if he's in on the theft, why was Markuss at the funeral home? He took his wife to water aerobics." Cam grunted. "A class like that's probably only an hour long. It could've been over before I even left Paul Bearer's last night. Still, he went back. I wonder why." The microwave beeped.

Cam retrieved his soup and sat at a corner of the dining table. To Bait, he said, "Whether or not there was an outsider involved, there had to be at least one insider if the cooler was locked. Let's see if I can winnow down the list. Did all seven know that Mrs. Bitter was wearing an expensive necklace? Blair knew, of course, because she worked on the body. Same with Markuss. Kacey told me Mitzy knew. And I'd be surprised if

Samir didn't know, too. But what about Piper, Shane, and Jelly Roll? Would they have seen Mrs. Bitter before the memorial service?" Cam lowered his head. "Kacey said the ruby was listed in the ledger. I wonder if they all knew where that was kept."

He closed his eyes. "Some of Mrs. Bitter's family members surely knew she was wearing the necklace. But they wouldn't know the code to the mortuary cooler. No, Bait, my gut tells me this was an inside job. Either Samir or Markuss got mixed up with the wrong partner or one of Paul Bearer's workers did the deed himself."

He jerked his head up and snapped open his eyelids. "Or herself. Bait, did you see the hilt of the blade in Samir? No, of course you didn't. I didn't appreciate it when I saw Samir's body lying prone on the carpet, but I'm sure the handle of that knife was pointed upward. Someone shorter than Samir must have stabbed him."

Chapter 6

"Where were you yesterday?" Samantha Krause shouted, the moment Cam set foot in Peachy Kleen's office. Strands of frosted hair sprang from her tight bun like an upended jellyfish.

"Sorry, I was at Paul Bearer's almost the entire day, and without my phone."

Samantha's hand shot to her mouth. "Omigosh! I saw your name next to the job on the schedule for Monday. Were you there when Samir was killed?"

"No." Cam flopped onto the comfortable sofa in the "bullpen." Samantha stood behind him, fixing coffee at the rear of the office's central room. "How did you hear about Samir?"

"How did I hear?" Samantha huffed. "It's all anyone can talk about. So, if you cleaned Paul Bearer's on Monday, why were you there yesterday?"

"I got off to a late start on Monday, then because of the storm had to go back to do the apartment. I never did make it up there. Samir was killed between the time I left and came back." He filled her in on the day's events, other than finding the roofies.

"You're a suspect?" Samantha asked with a tone of disbelief, handing Cam a cup of black coffee. "Right silly that is. Bernie has no sense." She plopped down onto the sofa beside him. The cushions bounced, sending a wave of joe onto his lap. Cam winced as it pierced his jeans and scalded his inner thigh. He kept his mouth shut and shifted to the left—Samantha commanded twice as much sofa space as him.

"So, what are you going to do about it?" she asked and raised her own coffee cup to her lips with a pinky stabbing the air—a queenly gesture from the woman in peacock-print leggings.

"What am I going to do?" Cam repeated. "Bury my head in a line in the sand and hope Chief Leftwich doesn't arrest me, I suppose."

"No, no!" Samantha boomed and sprang to her feet in a single, remarkably fluid, motion. Cam lifted his bottom an inch from the sofa cushion to stabilize his mug and avoid a second spill. "*You* have to find the murderer," she said. "It's the only way to make sure your name is cleared. We can't have you getting shipped up-river."

There weren't any rivers running up through Rusted Bonnet, or down it for that matter, but Cam had to admit she was probably right. Besides, he'd relished the rush of solving the village's only other murder in recent history. To Samantha, he said, "I can't imagine I'll be able to learn anything more than the police, but it might not hurt to try."

"You need to put the pedal to the metal, Cam."

"And hit the deck running. Got it." Of course, he wasn't quite sure even where to start.

***

"It's a real life treasure hunt," Becka Blom said in a manner void of enthusiasm but spiked with a hint of interest. The sable-skinned housekeeper handed Cam an envelope with a flip of her wrist. Becka and her mother, Malika, had arrived at the bullpen just minutes after Samantha departed.

"What is?" Cam asked and accepted the envelope.

"A letter from a lawyer," Becka groaned.

"A letter from your father, you mean," Malika said and lowered herself onto the sofa, which was quickly reaching threadbare status. "Delivered by a lawyer."

The previous year, Becka had discovered that her father—then deceased for two years—had kidnapped her as a toddler and whisked her away from her mother in Kenya to a port city in South Africa for the duration of her childhood. They later moved to Rusted Bonnet where he—a skilled welder of large ships—had found a position with a company servicing vessels that traversed the Great Lakes. Only recently had Becka—known to her mother as Afya—and Malika reunited. Cam was fortunate enough to now have both women on the Peachy Kleen payroll.

Cam lifted the envelope's flap and examined its contents. The first page was dated seven years earlier and addressed to an attorney based in Knysna, South Africa. Signed by Gakuru "Gak" Blom—Becka's father and Malika's ex-husband—it dictated that the attached letter was to be provided to his daughter one year after his death or on her twenty-fifth birthday, whichever came later. Cam sat on the opposite end of the sofa from Malika and turned to the next page.

"Dearest, Becka," it began. "I have a confession to make. One for which you may never forgive me...." The letter proceeded to explain, in painstaking detail, that he had taken her from her mother when she was three-years-old and that, as of the writing of the letter, her mother was still alive. The information wouldn't be news for Becka or Malika now, though reading it still tore at Cam's insides. But no tears came to his eyes. The words seemed cold rather than heartfelt.

He looked up at Becka. Bags pooled under her eyes. Becka answered his unasked question. "I still haven't forgiven him," she said. "Mom and Missy have had to endure more of my emotional rollercoasters than I ever thought imaginable." Cam knew that Missy Graves was Becka's girlfriend. "I had always thought of my father so fondly. That he was so strong to have raised me by himself. And he was a good father to me." She shook her head sideways. "Enough emotion. Keep reading—get past the confession part."

Cam continued. Midway down the next page, he read:

While nothing can bring back the years you lost with your mother, I have a gift for you. When you were still a child, I refurbished the Durban Destiny—a magnificent ship. A fellow welder was a member of a dive crew that scavenged sunken ships for salvage. His crew located a ship on the floor of the Southern Ocean eighty miles south of Port Elizabeth. Given the state of the wreck and its location, it matched news clippings of the sinking of the Jaffna Clipper—a fast boat sailing from Sri Lanka to Cape Town that sank in 1851.

My colleague and his crew offered me and nine others working the Destiny a chance to invest in their effort to reclaim the treasures of the Clipper. Sri Lankan newspapers had estimated that the boat contained hundreds—if not thousands—of kilos of silver.

I leapt at the opportunity and it paid off. For 35,000 Rand, I was given a percentage of all valuables recovered from the Clipper. It was the best investment I ever made! The dive crew unearthed an enormous chest of silver. My share amounted to three massive bars, each weighing about 30 kilos.

Cam glanced at Becka, who was leaning against the door to

the storage room. "How much is a Rand worth in dollars?" he asked.

"I've done the math. 35,000 Rand is $2,500. Right now, silver is worth about $500 per kilo."

"How many pounds are in a kilo?" Cam asked.

"I believe 2.2. So, the bars are each about 66 pounds. Worth about $15,000 each. Forty-five thousand all together. Even more if the price of silver goes up." A tiny smile cracked her lips.

"Or less if it goes down," Malika commented.

"The bars are for you?" Cam asked Becka.

She pointed at the letter still in Cam's hand. He read.

"The silver bars are yours to keep, Becka. They are inside a safe deposit box at the Absa bank branch in the Garden Route Center here in Knysna under my name. My attorney can provide you a key. Love, Daddy."

"It doesn't seem like too much of a treasure hunt," Cam said.

"Oh, yes it is," Malika said and removed another envelope from her handbag. "This is a second letter from Gak that the lawyer—one here in Rusted Bonnet—gave Becka." She unfolded it and read.

"Since moving to the United States, I have decided to move the silver bars as well. I asked my lawyer in Knysna to ship them here. Mr. Oso Thibodaux, Esq. maintains a vault in his office for his clients. He has all of the necessary paperwork from me for you to retrieve them."

"This Oso Thibodaux was your father's lawyer here? He gave you these letters?" Cam asked.

"Yes," Becka said. "The problem is, he doesn't have the silver bars."

"What?" Cam shot to his feet. "How's that possible?"

"My dearest daddy didn't pay his bills. I only got these letters from Mr. Thibodaux because after daddy died, I paid off his debts from what he had in his estate. An estate that left me with no inheritance. Or so I thought until this morning."

"Today's your birthday?"

Becka smiled. "Number twenty-five. My mother and Missy are taking me to get tapas tonight."

"Happy birthday," Cam said. "So, what happened to the silver?"

"According to Mr. Thibodaux, Gak retrieved them before he could sell a bar and recoup the costs he was owed," Malika said. "None of us has any idea what my rocks for brains ex-husband did with them."

"But," Becka chimed in, "the lawyer says that if we can find them, they're mine."

***

If Cam hadn't known that Chet Szubek hailed from Rusted Bonnet, he would've pegged the fit, twenty-something-year-old as the product of a Long Island prep school and the Ivy Leagues: a salmon-colored Vineyard Vines polo with a popped collar complimented oversized aviators perched along his hairline, dark jeans, and brown flip flops.

When Cam sauntered into the Bear Claw—a popular diner in the village—for lunch, he recognized Chet by sight. As a standout hockey player, his photograph had been splattered all over the local papers years earlier. Now, propped up on a red vinyl-covered stool at the breakfast bar in front of a well-worked grill, his chiseled jaw and dark mop stood out. *His feet must be freezing in those flip flops,* Cam thought.

Cam slid onto a stool, leaving an open one between himself and Chet, and ordered a Monte Cristo and iced tea. He handed the waitress two slices of sourdough sealed in a Ziploc bag.

Chet shot him a quizzical look.

"I have celiac disease," Cam explained. He and Chet were

the only patrons at the counter. "Gluten makes my intestines go crazy, so I bring my own bread. I've been around long enough that the waitresses don't bat an eyelash."

"I thought gluten-free was a diet," Chet said and looked down at his French dip.

"I wish. For me, it's everyday life. Are you here for work or just visiting?" Cam asked, despite knowing the reason.

"I used to live here," Chet replied without looking up.

"And where are you now?" Cam asked, unwilling to be brushed off.

Chet sighed and looked at him. "Chicago. My grandfather died. His funeral was yesterday."

"I'm sorry." Cam suspected Chet didn't know who he was. "At Paul Bearer's or the other one, the Catholic home?"

Chet harrumphed, then said, "You didn't hear?"

Cam shook his head, playing dumb.

"Samir Orucov, the owner of Paul Bearer's, died himself the other night. F'ing murdered if you can believe it. The place is a crime scene, so they shipped Grandpa's body over to the Catholic place."

"That must have been tough," Cam said.

"No big deal. They were able to accommodate us and we're not exactly a religious family. And Mitzy … I mean, Mrs. Orucov, made it easy enough." Chet's cheeks colored when he mentioned Mitzy's name.

"Do you know her well?" Cam asked.

Chet shook his head vigorously. "Not at all."

***

Cam spent the early afternoon hours paired with Tabby Vazquez, a woman in her mid-forties with a pair of teenagers, cleaning a townhouse on the western side of the village. After finishing, as they were loading supplies into the van he'd dubbed "Montana," Cam noticed Piper Quick, across the street stepping out of a door and onto a porch.

The redhead was dressed in faded blue jeans and a baggy Western Michigan sweatshirt. She lit a cigarette and took a long drag.

"Why don't you take Montana back to the office," Cam said to Tabby and snapped shut the back door to the van. "The air's refreshing and most of the sidewalks have been shoveled."

Tabby squinted at him.

"Even if any aren't clear," he added, "the streets between here and downtown have been plowed."

"Suit yourself," Tabby said. "Becka and I still have the Kennesaw job so I need to get back and pick her up." She lifted herself into the van and took off.

Cam made eye contact with Piper and gave her a small wave. She smiled in recognition and Cam crossed the street.

"I didn't realize you cleaned Mrs. Sparrow's place," Piper said and laid her cigarette in an ashtray on the railing. Her porch was cheaply decorated. A plastic Christmas wreath had been tacked by a single nail to the door above a mat adorned with paw prints. A feathered dreamcatcher lifelessly hung from the ceiling.

Cam planted a foot on the bottom of three steps leading up to the porch. "My company's been cleaning it for a while, but today's the first time I've been here. I usually have two of the gals do it. I didn't know you lived here."

"For seventeen years," Piper said. "Not that I'm ever here on a weekday afternoon. It's too quiet. Disconcerting."

"Mitzy hasn't given you the go ahead to come back?"

Piper shook her head. "I guess the police haven't allowed it." She looked down at her cigarette. "I'm not sure if I'm ever going back."

"Why's that?"

"I have a feeling Mitzy's going to sell the place." She scratched her cheek. "I suppose the new owner might want me. I know the place better than anyone else now that Samir's gone." She gave him a crooked smile.

Cam stubbed a toe against the side of a porch step. A clump of dirty snow slopped to the ground. "I hadn't even thought about who might run the home. I suppose Mitzy's not exactly up to the task."

Piper stifled a laugh. "That's for sure. The woman was so drunk on Monday night, she didn't even hear her own husband get stabbed. She must've been passed out. The place isn't a gem, but Mitzy should get a pretty enough penny." She picked her cigarette back up. "Enough to support her Bacardi habit."

"Do you get along with her?"

Piper turned up her lips, showing yellowed teeth. "Sure, why not," she said breezily. "Mistress of the manor. She doesn't treat us peasants poorly as long as we keep the bodies moving in and out and she doesn't have to lift a finger." She took a puff and turned her head to blow smoke away from Cam. "The woman's smarter than I am—to land a man like Samir and just coast."

"Do you have any idea why someone would want to kill him?" Cam asked.

Piper's eyes darted from Cam's gaze. "A robbery gone bad is what I heard. The deputy stopped by. She's your ex-wife, right?"

Cam nodded. "I haven't spoken to her since yesterday. Did she happen to say whether Markuss had recovered?"

"It was the first thing I asked her." Tears welled in Piper's eyes. "Markuss is an old space cadet, but always so kind."

Space cadet? "He didn't make it?" Cam shoved his hands in his jeans pockets.

Piper sniffled and lifted the bottom of her sweatshirt to dab her eyes, showing off a porcelain midriff. "No, sorry, he'll be fine. Deputy Gingerfield said the wound didn't go deep enough to hit anything vital. It was more of a graze than anything, thank goodness. I'm going to visit him later this afternoon."

That's an excellent idea, Cam thought. To Piper, he said, "I don't suppose he saw his attacker."

"If only the police had been so lucky. The deputy said he never saw it coming."

After another minute of small talk, Cam bade Piper goodbye. As he stepped onto the sidewalk, the front door of the townhouse two doors down from Piper's flew open and Blair Lamb jetted out, a smart phone jammed to one ear. She jogged to a black hatchback, climbed inside, and sped off without so much as looking in Cam's direction.

***

Had Blair been visiting someone or did she live there? Later, sitting on a built-in bench in his shower, scrubbing the soles of his feet with a stiff brush, Cam pondered the import of seeing Blair. By the time he'd turned to ask Piper, she had disappeared inside.

Cam stepped out of the shower, a sheet of cold smacking his chest. He quickly wrapped a towel around his waist and checked the bedroom clock—four o'clock, plenty of time to visit Markuss in the hospital and do a bit of investigating.

A *ding* sounded from Cam's phone. A text from Kacey—"the chief wants to interview you. 9 a.m. Tomorrow at the station." He groaned.

The doorbell chimed as Cam slunk into a pair of brown cords and a half-zip sweater. He hopped down the steps and peered out of the front door peephole: Mitzy Orucov was cramming a stick of pink chewing gum into her mouth. He opened the door.

"Hi, Cam," Mitzy said, bouncing on her toes in black stilettos and a tight-fitting skirt that barely reached her knees. Not exactly practical winter wear.

"Come in, Mitzy. You must be freezing."

She toddled inside, smacking the gum in her mouth. "I saw the sun and thought it was warm outside," she said.

Cam led her to a stool in front of the granite countertop in his kitchen. "Can I get you something to warm up? Coffee? Tea?"

"Coffee if you have the Bailey's."

Cam didn't have an ounce of liquor in his kitchen, just beer and wine. "Sorry," he said. "I don't."

Mitzy rubbed her hands together. "Hot tea, then. Thank you."

Cam rummaged in his lower kitchen cabinets for a kettle. "How are you holding up?" he asked.

"I am doing so-so." She sighed. "Stay positive is what I say —here is the change I need to liven up my life. Samir was a roommate, not a lover."

"Will it be hard to find a new funeral director for Paul Bearer's?" Cam filled the kettle with water and set it on a burner.

Mitzy waved her fingers dismissively. "I have no interest in this business of the dead. And Shaney-boy cannot take it over. Not enough brains. Even if he would probably like to—how do you say?—give it a shot."

"You won't let him try?"

She harrumphed. "He would run the place into ruin. I will never get more for the place than I can right now."

Cam set a small wooden box overflowing with tea bags in front of Mitzy. She selected Lemon Zinger and said, "I like these, the herbal teas. Very fruity! I'm thinking about moving back to Baku."

"And Shane?"

"No chance he will want to come with me, thank goodness.

He is an American idiot through and through." She raised a hand. "I should not say that. America is a great country. Little Shane just couldn't take advantage of the school system."

"He's no rocket surgeon?"

"Ha! You know that is true. I would not be surprised if he still wears Superman Underoos for adults. I will ask whoever buys Paul Bearer's to let him continue to deliver the death certificates. He does that for the Catholic place, too."

Cam poured hot water into a tea cup and set it on a saucer in front of Mitzy. He poured another for himself and added a bag of oolong. "Have the police allowed you to resume business?" Cam asked despite having asked Piper a similar question just an hour earlier.

"Tomorrow. We missed only the two services on Tuesday. Today was one viewing. The funeral game is all last-minute business." She slid a saucy grin in Cam's direction.

Cam returned an awkward smile. "I only saw two bodies when I was there on Monday."

"The one for today was cremated. That is the way to go for a woman—one last chance for a smoking hot body!" Mitzy laughed and touched her tongue to her upper lip.

Cam had to admit to himself that Mitzy had a good bit of sex appeal. He ground his front teeth into his lower lip, then said, "I ran into Mr. Szubek's grandson at the Bear Claw this morning. He said the Catholic place was able to accommodate his grandfather."

"They were only too happy to get our business," Mitzy clucked. "You saw him this morning? So silly little Chet decided to stick around."

Silly little Chet? "He told me he's staying through the weekend. He figured as long as he was here, he might as well spend some time with his parents and catch up with some old friends."

Mitzy's eyes flashed fire. "Hmm...."

"Do you know Chet well?" Cam asked.

"Hardly," she said loudly.

An almost identical response to the one Chet had at the mention of Mitzy's name.

"Samir and I used to be friends with his parents, that is all," she added quickly.

"Used to be?"

"We grew apart. Even friends do that sometimes."

Chapter 7

Delphi Hospital was undoubtedly a product of the 1960s: tiled walls with black and white photos stared down at orderlies wheeling aluminum carts.

A desk attendant in a white nurse's cap directed Cam to Markuss's room. He knocked on a closed door and a woman's voice echoed, "Come in," from inside.

Markuss lay on his stomach, facing the door, on a metal-framed hospital bed. A chalky white sheet covered him from neck to foot. Next to his bed, in a wooden chair, sat a woman with tight gray curls screwed into her head and a dog-eared copy of *Anna Karenina* in her lap.

Markuss's shaggy eyebrows narrowed at the sight of Cam. "I recognize you," he rasped. "You helped me move Szubek to the cooler."

"I did," Cam said, stepping inside.

"I'm Markuss's wife, Jana," the woman said—pronouncing the name, 'Yana'—and stood to shake Cam's hand. Her grip was non-existent. She sat back down and set the book on a small table beside her. "Do you work at Paul Bearer's or the

Catholic place?"

"Neither," Cam replied and shut the door behind him. "I own the housekeeping company that cleans Paul Bearer's. I ran into Markuss on Monday afternoon, before he took you to water aerobics."

Jana grinned. "Such a puerile class, but good fun."

Cam took a step closer to the bed. "How are you feeling?"

"I've been better," Markuss replied. "But seeing as how I was knifed in the back less than forty-eight hours ago, I can't complain. Too bad I never saw the ... bugger who tried to ram it into me."

"Did you feel him pull it out?" Cam asked.

"I'm not sure it was ever in. The doctor said it was more of a slash. Not that it matters; I must have fainted or something. I lost consciousness right away." He crinkled his nose; its skin was chapped. "But how'd you know it wasn't sticking out of me?"

"I went back to the funeral home on Tuesday morning to clean the upstairs apartment. I was one of the first people who found you."

"You must be Cam Reddick," Jana said. "Your name came up on my Caller ID when Mitzy called with the news."

"She borrowed my phone," Cam said to Jana then turned his attention back to Markuss. "I was surprised to see you on Tuesday morning." He held up a hand. "Not just because you'd been attacked, but because of the storm on Monday night. Why'd you go back to Paul Bearer's?"

"The police asked me the same thing," Markuss grumbled. "I forgot my wallet."

Cam raised an eyebrow.

"I empty my pockets before embalming a body," he explained. "Before I left to drive Jana, I managed to pick up my keys, phone, and jack knife, but I forgot the cursed thing. I didn't realize it until just before I went to bed. So, I schlepped myself back to the home at an ungodly hour."

To Jana, Cam asked, "You didn't notice that Markuss didn't come home?"

Jana's lips puckered. "I'm a sound sleeper. In fact, I was still in bed when Mitzy called."

Markuss coughed—it sounded phlegmy and wet. "You ask a lot of questions, young man. Why exactly are you here?"

Cam looked at the floor. "I wanted to make sure you were all right."

"And?" the older man asked. *Definitely not a space cadet as Piper had described him.*

"A-and," Cam stammered, looking back up. "The chief is on my case because I didn't leave Paul Bearer's until seven o'clock on Monday night and no one saw me go."

Jana's eyes peeled open wide. "You're a suspect?"

"Not a real one," Cam said, knowing he had to report to the police station the following morning to be interviewed.

She pointed at the door. "You'd better leave or I'm calling security."

"Just please tell me," Cam said to Markuss, "what time did you get back to the funeral home on Monday night?"

Jana's eyes flashed white. "By leave, I mean now!"

***

Cam squeezed onto a stool at the S-shaped bar between a wiry man in an old-school bowler hat and a boxy woman sucking on the bone of a chicken wing. The Stagger Inn served as Rusted Bonnet's go-to drinking establishment for anyone over the age of thirty.

Cam ordered a Founders All Day IPA and swung around to survey the patrons. In a village as small as Rusted Bonnet, chances were high he'd spot someone he knew.

Shane and Jelly Roll were hunched over a table near an orange brick fireplace. Small flames crackled from imitation wood. Cam grabbed his beer and made his way to their table, crunching peanut shells that covered the floor.

"Mind if I join you?" he asked, pulling out a chair that faced the front of the bar.

"Why not?" Jelly Roll said, pushing up the sleeves of a crewneck sweater. A dark thatch of growth beneath his chin matched the forest of hair on his forearms.

Cam set his beer on a coaster and sat facing Shane. "Sorry about your father."

Shane sniffed, then jutted his brow. "He was a fine dad. But there comes a time when you have to become the man of the family." He drank from a pint glass and wiped the back of his hand across his mouth. Traces of foam caught in his mutton chops.

"By taking care of your mother?" Cam ventured.

"And the home." He motioned to a waitress for another beer.

"I suppose you and Mitzy must have talked about the future quite a bit during the last couple of days," Cam said, knowing that Mitzy planned to sell Paul Bearer's and possibly even move back to Azerbaijan.

"Not yet," Shane grunted. "But I got it figured out. Mom can keep the apartment. Me and Jelly'll take over Paul Bearer's. But we're definitely getting a nicer place to live. Probably something here in the village. Royal Oak is too far." He tossed a peanut into the fireplace.

"Thas' for sure," Jelly Roll added. "I told the folks at the Cath-lic place I was done there. Won't have time to drive that hearse for 'em anymore."

"You shouldn't count your chickens before they come home to roost," Cam said under his breath.

The waitress handed Shane a glass filled with beer the color of maple syrup. "Can I get you fellas anything to eat?" she asked the three men.

As Jelly Roll jabbed a stubby finger at a laminated menu, Cam watched Blair Lamb stride into the Stagger. She unzipped a puffy black winter jacket to reveal a fitted pink sweater and skinny jeans, then crunched in Tony Lama cowboy boots to the end of the bar.

Shane reached across the table and poked Cam in the ribs. "Think I'll have a shot with Blair once she sees me running Paul Bearer's?" he whispered.

The waitress departed and Jelly Roll ratcheted his neck, following Shane's line of vision. "That girl sure is fine."

"Dibs," Shane said. "I'm, like, her boss now."

"You might want to be careful of sexual harassment," Cam said.

Shane audibly gulped a swallow of beer. "We don't work in some cubicle farm. No one cares about that kind of stuff around here."

Cam suppressed his impulse to smack the louse. Instead, he asked, "How can you be sure your mother won't sell Paul Bearer's?"

Shane's face twisted into a pretzel. "W-why would she want to do that?" he sputtered.

Cam didn't answer.

Shane glanced at Jelly Roll, then looked back at Cam with hardened eyes. "No way I'm letting her sell. It's mine."

***

Cam waited patiently for a series of men to try their luck with Blair. She allotted each no more than five minutes before sending them packing. Cam glided onto a stool vacated by a disappointed-looking Asian with a shaved head and tortoise shell hipster glasses, then asked the bartender for a glass of ice water and turned his attention to Blair. Dark lavender lipstick smudged the rim of her almost-empty sangria glass.

"I saw you this afternoon," Cam said.

Blair's marscaraed eyelashes flickered. "Hi, Cam. Where, at AutoZone?"

"No. I had a job on Fisher. Piper was on her porch when I finished so I popped over for a chat. I saw you leave the townhouse a couple of doors down. Are you two neighbors?"

"We are." She tucked a swath of coffee-colored hair behind one ear. "I had no idea Piper lived nearby until after I moved in a couple of years ago. Not that we hang out or anything."

"Is Samir's death going to hurt your business?" Cam asked as the bartender slid a glass of water in front of him.

"Why should it? I don't know of another cosmetologist for miles who's willing to slap Smoky Rose on a corpse's lips. So, I imagine I'll keep getting the local business. How about you— do you expect to keep the place as a client?"

The question hadn't even crossed Cam's mind. He told Blair as much, then added, "I'd hate to lose the place, but we have almost a hundred regulars so it wouldn't be the end of the world."

Blair tilted her head to one side. "A hundred? I had no idea. Do you own the company now or is that still your mother?"

"I do. Since I moved back to Rusted Bonnet last year."

Blair didn't respond right away. She appeared to be thinking. After taking a sip of Sangria, she said, "You're single now, right?"

Cam nodded. With the exception of an evening at a French bistro with Kacey followed by ice skating, he hadn't dated anyone since moving back to Rusted Bonnet. A corner of his heart held out hope of reconciliation with Kacey—more than the co-parenting arrangement they had now. Cam had thoroughly enjoyed their night out together and he believed Kacey had, too. But she'd declined his invitation to hike and picnic the following weekend, saying she just wasn't ready to dive back in.

Cam sipped his water in silence while Blair finished her drink. *She was neither flirting with him nor pushing him away,* Cam thought. More like sizing him up.

"Can I get you another glass of Sangria?" he offered.

"No, thank you." She waved to the bartender. "May I have my bill, please?" Blair opened an expensive-looking handbag that was hanging off the back of her chair. She fished around inside.

Cam's eyes naturally gravitated toward the open bag. As she pulled out a leather wallet, he spotted a flash of foil. A second later, Blair snapped the bag shut. But Cam could swear he'd just seen a packet of the same green pills he'd found in the funeral home.

Chapter 8

Thursday, February 11

Cam exhaled loudly. Bernie Leftwich's interrogation style ricocheted from shouting to growling to mocking, all while heaving blanket accusations. When the chief finally left the village police station's interview room, Cam felt like he'd gone ten rounds with a gorilla saddled by a chip on his shoulder.

Minutes later, Kacey stole into the bare room and handed Cam a plastic cup of water. She closed the door and sat down across from him at a metal table.

"You survived," she said with a smile.

"Barely," Cam said weakly. "He sure had a beef to pick with me. He must have said 'I know you did it' a half dozen times."

"Sorry about that." Kacey placed a manila folder on the table in front of her. "He thinks guilty people fold when they're confronted. I've never seen it happen. If anything, direct accusations make people clam up."

"What's in the folder?" Cam asked.

"Samir's police record from New Jersey. Cam, what can you

tell me about Piper Quick?"

His eyes bore down on the closed folder, but he couldn't will it open. Cam looked up at Kacey after a moment. "I spoke with Piper yesterday. She lives across the street from one of my clients and I saw her on her porch. Did you know she lives two doors down from Blair Lamb?"

"Yes. I spoke with both of them in their homes."

"Of course," Cam said. "What do I know about Piper? She told me she's been living there for seventeen years. Though I'm not sure how long she's been with Paul Bearer's. I never spoke much with her when I was cleaning. But she seemed more distraught over Samir's death than Mitzy did."

"And do you think that grief is genuine?"

Cam's eyebrows rocketed upward. "You don't?"

Kacey didn't answer the question. Instead, she asked, "What about Piper's interactions with Markuss? While you were cleaning, did you notice whether they spent much time together?"

"On Monday?"

"Not just then. Any time you were in the home."

Cam took some time to consider the question, then answered, "Not particularly. On occasion, I heard them discussing schedules—when a body needed to be embalmed for a particular service."

"Was it professional conversation or more familiar? Like you and Darby?"

Cam's right eye twitched. "You think Markuss is Piper's father?"

Kacey looked down at the folder. "I probably said too much." She lowered her voice. "You were so kind helping me navigate my crazy ideas on the last murder case that I keep forgetting you're a suspect."

"Other than sitting in the interrogation room here, of course."

"Of course."

"Kacey, come on," Cam pleaded. He took a sip of water. "We're not being recorded in here, are we?"

Kacey shook her head.

"Let me be your sounding board. You *know* I had nothing to do with this."

"I do," Kacey whispered. "Actually, I tried to talk Bernie out of bringing you in for more questioning."

"You're not worried that I could've seen the combination when Markuss opened the cooler?"

Kacey smiled. "You picked up on that?"

"Eventually."

"I never thought you were involved. But I had to do everything by the book."

"And now?"

"I think the snow saved you."

Cam blinked away a speck of dust from his eye. "How so?"

Kacey folded her hands on the table. "Samir went to get gas. I checked his credit card. He made one purchase at the Valero at 7:25, and a second transaction there four minutes later. I found the guy who was on shift. He knew Samir by sight and recalled him pumping gas into a plastic container. He paid for his gas at the pump then went inside for a Red Bull and snacks. Samir told him he needed fuel for his snow blower."

"That explains the two charges," Cam said.

"Yes. And the counterman's recollection is key—it wasn't someone else using Samir's card. Visa puts your grocery transaction from Alwards at 7:31." Kacey smiled. "Fortunate timing."

"So why on earth did the chief drag me down here? I should be at work."

"Because, technically, you could've come back after shopping and killed Samir." Kacey held up her hands. "His words not mine. Forensics put the time of Samir's death sometime between 7:30 and 8:30 on Monday night. So, you're still theoretically a suspect, but it's strained. Bernie probably just wanted to lay into you." She sighed. "It might've been easier for *me* if it hadn't snowed on Monday night. If the killer left any tire tracks or footprints, they were covered by the time I arrived."

Cam's mind flashed to the funeral home's snowy parking lot on Tuesday morning. "Wait a minute. When I arrived on Tuesday, there was only one car in the lot other than Mitzy's and Samir's. And the police cars, of course. But both Piper and Markuss were inside."

"It was Piper's," Kacey explained. "Markuss parked his Cadillac in the street near the garage."

"I wonder why."

"He said he always went in through the back. It's closer to the prep room and that's where he left his wallet, which is why he'd gone back to the home."

"How's he doing?"

"He was released from the hospital this morning. His lesion was largely superficial and the doctors think he'll be as good as new in a week." Kacey pursed her lips together. "Can I bounce something off of you?"

Cam nodded.

She tapped her nails against the manila folder. "The state of New Jersey never took Samir to trial. But he was arrested there. According to his file," she said looking down, "his lawyer struck a plea and all he got was a short stint of parole."

"He did time in Kansas, though," Cam stated.

"Yes, for pumping sawdust into feed bags. It looks like he had something more complex going on in Cape May. That's the town in Jersey."

"Something related to Markuss and Piper?"

"I'm not sure. It's just a hunch. Do you know what check washing is?"

"Another term for forgery?" Cam ventured. He clasped his hands together on the table.

"Almost, but not exactly. It's when someone erases the details of a check and rewrites it. But there's no forging the signature. According to Bernie, it was a fairly common con before people started using credit cards to pay for everything. It's pretty simple —nail polish remover can take off almost any ink from paper. Rubbing alcohol works, too."

"I had no idea."

"Well, the Cape May P.D. was pretty sure Samir was an expert. According to the file, they thought he was running a scam centered around mortgage payments. Back then, most homeowners sent their bank a monthly check—they just stuck it in the outgoing mail. Samir would target an upscale home in an area without much foot traffic. That way, he could check the mailbox before the carrier came without being noticed. Outgoing mortgage checks would be pretty easy to spot—people didn't send letters to their bank for much else. When he saw one, he'd just take it and that homeowner became his prey. Samir would wash off the name of the bank and write in his own, then cash the check. He monitored his victims' boxes after the mail was dropped off, too, and trash any delinquency letters. The banks did Samir a favor and usually marked them 'Past Due' in bright red on the outside of the envelope. He could steal five or six payments from a mark before the bank's foreclosure department started calling, which would tip off the homeowner."

"That's pretty ingenious."

"Six mortgage payments on a $300,000 house could've been as much as eight or nine grand."

Cam whistled. "He'd have to swipe statements, too, I imagine. Otherwise, wouldn't the homeowner know the bank wasn't depositing the checks?"

"Samir had that angle covered. He set up a corporate front—Gilman Mortgage Processing. After he washed the checks, he made them out to the company, not himself personally. So, if the homeowner looked at his statement, he'd just assume the bank had started using a processing company. And the dollars drawn from the account matched the amount of the check they wrote, so it wasn't likely to raise suspicion. Of course, Samir used false identification to set up the account, and as Gilman's sole employee, he removed the cash from it almost as soon as it came in the door."

"How'd he get caught?"

"One of the homeowners went to the bank. The police notes say he was depositing a ten-dollar birthday check from his ninety year-old grandmother. The bank manager pulled the man aside to ask if he needed any assistance. He'd made every mortgage payment on time for eight years, then 'missed' four straight."

Cam cleared his throat. "So why was there a plea bargain?"

"Apparently, the link between Samir and Gilman was too weak for the prosecutor to take to a jury."

"Wow," Cam said. He rubbed his eyes. "And where do Markuss and Piper fit in?"

"I'm not sure if they do. The only file Cape May police could find after all of these years isn't exactly robust." She held up the manila envelope. "It has an officer's handwritten notes on the con and victims, but there's no typed report. The officer retired years ago and the detective I spoke with said anything they had on paper would've been scanned into this file when they upgraded to their electronic records system."

Kacey opened the folder and handed Cam the top sheet of paper. "Look near the bottom. Where I highlighted."

Cam surveyed the document—a photocopy of a sheet of lined

paper with scratchy cursive. Five lines from the bottom, emblazoned in neon yellow, he read to himself: "Vics: M.O./ T.L. + 2 (children), E.S.A., M.V. + P.V. (child)."

"M.V. and P.V.?" Cam asked.

"That's what I saw. M.V. could be Markuss Vitolins and P.V., Piper. She goes by Quick, of course, and has for as long as I've known her. But you never know."

"Could Quick be a married name that she kept after a divorce?"

"I checked the records here in town and didn't see evidence of a marriage, but that doesn't mean she didn't change her name before moving to Rusted Bonnet."

Cam stood up. "What about Jana? The notes don't list a J.V."

"She wasn't in the picture back then."

"You asked him about this?"

"Yes, all of it. An hour ago. He said M.V. isn't him." Kacey drummed her fingers on the table. "According to Markuss, he's never lived in New Jersey and is childless. He said that he and Jana got hitched later in life—fifteen years ago. It was a first marriage for each of them."

"Did you ask him about Piper?"

"Not by name. Just whether he had a daughter."

"But you don't believe him?" Cam said and rocked his chair back against a bare wall.

"I don't know," Kacey replied. "I don't see why I shouldn't. M.V. is a common enough set of initials."

Cam nodded his head. "Piper said she's been living here for seventeen years. Let's say she and Markuss moved to Rusted Bonnet to carry out a little vigilante justice. They get jobs at the funeral home to be in close proximity to Samir. Why wait so long to kill him? Plus, if Piper is Markuss's daughter and they tag teamed the murder, why would she attack her own father?"

"Good questions," Kacey said. "Very good questions."

Chapter 9

"We have a moral dilemma," Samantha Krause declared.

Elbows-deep in paperwork, Cam was curled into his desk chair inside the "breadbox"—his tiny office within Peachy Kleen's quarters in the heart of Rusted Bonnet. He looked up to see Samantha's figure filling the door frame. He could hear someone rustling about behind her—most likely Tabby Vazquez, whom she was paired with for the day.

Cam pushed aside a stack of supply invoices. "We, meaning you and me?"

Samantha shook her head. A lock of hair shook loose from an eggplant-shaped mass mounted atop her head. In a single, deft motion, she curled it around a finger and nestled it back into place—like a momma bird feeding her baby a worm. "We meaning Tabby and me. Well, at least that's the first dilemma. There's a second one and that involves you."

Cam rose. Despite the eight-foot-high ceiling, every time he stood upright in the breadbox he felt claustrophobic. "That makes as much sense as a book on how to read."

Samantha trilled and turned. Cam followed her into the

bullpen. The coffee grinder in the kitchenette revved. "Want a cup, boss?" Tabby asked without turning around.

"That sounds great. But stop calling me boss, please."

Tabby shrugged her shoulders.

"Start at the beginning," Cam said to Samantha and leaned against a wall.

"It's like this," Samantha said. "Tabby and I had the Galax place over on Commissary Avenue this morning. They have ferrets—the basement stinks to high heaven."

Cam smiled. He never scheduled himself to clean the Galax house with its powerful stench—one perk of scheduling the shifts. "They've been customers for a couple of years," he said. Cam had only been operating Peachy Kleen for eleven months but was well versed with his clients' longevity from Darby's meticulous records.

"Respectable folks. Or so I thought."

Cam waited patiently.

"Double moral dilemma there is," Samantha said.

He groaned.

Tabby handed Cam a mug of black coffee, then brought one laden with Splenda to Samantha. "There's no dilemma in my mind," she said. "If you don't tell him, I will."

"Fine, fine," Samantha huffed. "You're right, of course. We can't keep a major heist a secret."

Cam's neck yawed and scalding coffee trickled over the brim and onto his palm. He grabbed the mug with his other hand and whipped the burning one to his mouth. The clutch in his brain popped—had Samantha found Mrs. Bitter's ruby necklace?

"What heist?" he asked.

"You don't know that there was any *heist*," mewed Tabby, who was typically reserved compared to her housekeeping counterpart.

"If my Oliver says there was one, then there was."

Samantha's adult son, Oliver, stumbled in and out of Rusted Bonnet to press his mother for money like Winnie the Pooh coming back to the honey pot.

"*What heist?*" Cam repeated.

"The power cord I was using for the vacuum went kaput halfway through the job," Samantha said. "At first, I thought there was a problem with the vacuum itself. Nope, I stuck its plug straight into the socket and it worked fine. But I need an extension cord to reach some areas." She threw her hands in the air. "I know I should've just told Tabby and run back here. There's an extra in the there." Her eyes shifted toward the supply closet. "But we've got three jobs today and I didn't want to give up my precious down time. *This time.* Now that's wasted, of course!"

Cam ventured a look at Tabby. She stood across from the sofa, a hip resting against the side of an ancient television.

"I went to the Galax's garage to look for a cord I could borrow," Samantha went on. "No luck. But then I remembered they have an attic."

"Which is off limits," Tabby added.

"Yes," Samantha moaned. "There's a note at the bottom of their client I.D. form. Of course, we don't carry those around for our regulars, but I knew they didn't want us to go up there."

"I remember seeing it when I reviewed the client files," Cam added. "It seemed a bit strange—it doesn't say, 'don't clean the attic;' more like 'please do not go into the attic'."

"That's right," Samantha said. "But I did." She cast her eyes toward the floor. "That's dilemma number one."

"Whether you should've gone up there?" Cam asked.

"No," Samantha said sheepishly. "Whether to tell you I disobeyed a client request."

"More like a client demand," Tabby said.

Samantha shot Tabby a wounded look. "I'm sorry, okay,"

Samantha said.

"If word gets out that we don't respect limits, Peachy Kleen will lose its customers and we'll be out of jobs," Tabby said.

"I know, I know." Tears beaded on the lower lids of Samantha's eyes. "And you have two boys at home. I get it. Cam, if you want me to resign, I will."

Cam pressed his forefingers into his temples. "I don't want you to resign, just don't ever do it again," he said. "Can we get back to this heist or whatever it is?"

"Yes, yes," Samantha said with a hint of relief in her voice. "So, I went into the attic. They have one of those pull-down staircases. I was scrounging around for an extension cord, when I came across something I've never seen before. It looked like a drying rack, but not quite. It was sturdier and with shelves, maybe seven or eight of them."

"To store paintings," Tabby said.

"Yes, there were three paintings, each laid flat on a shelf on top of some type of fancy paper and covered with a drop cloth. A dehumidifier was running on the floor next to the rack. No smell up there. I know I shouldn't have looked, but I was so curious! Such a sophisticated set up in the attic and it's not like Mr. or Mrs. Galax paint. Well, at least there's no studio or any art supplies that I've seen in the house."

"She thinks they're valuable," Tabby said.

"And stolen!" Samantha shrieked. "I lifted the cloth from one of the paintings to have a little peek. It looked like the Italian countryside to me, though it could have just as well been Indiana. But it was a right spectacle. I checked the other two and they were just as nice. Well, my Oliver has always been one to dilly about in museums and galleries, and like I said, I was curious."

"You called him to take a look?" Cam asked.

"No, I photographed the paintings with my phone,"

Samantha said and took a sip of her coffee. "After I emailed them to Oliver, I didn't expect to hear back from him so soon. I just wanted to know if he thought they were any good. He has an eye for that sort of thing—I don't see it myself. Why intelligent people pay thousands of dollars for paintings of blue dogs I'll never know!" She paused for breath, then re-launched. "The Galaxes did have an extension cord up there, so I left the paintings, and finished up the vacuuming downstairs. Well, low and behold, just as Tabby and I were loading up Georgia, Oliver sends me a message. It says, 'Mom, those look like Denys Roulands.' Well, I've never heard of the guy, but that doesn't mean diddly. So, I looked him up—he's a hotshot painter from the south of France!"

Cam shuffled to the kitchenette sink and set his empty coffee mug in it, then strode back to his spot against the wall. "So, the Galaxes purchased a few paintings. Why jump to the conclusion that they're stolen?"

"That's what I said," Tabby agreed.

"This Denys Rouland fella has an online gallery. Some of his paintings are listed at thirty to forty thousand Euros," Samantha countered. "Each! Why would anyone spend that kind of money and not hang them on a wall?"

"They bought the paintings as an investment and were worried about damage?" Cam ventured. "That would explain why they didn't want us going into the attic—minimize the risk."

"Pish tosh and a bottle of Pinosh," Samantha tutted. "If you spent that kind of money, you wouldn't stick them in your attic. They have special storage places you can rent in Bloomfield Hills. Mrs. Olszewski told me all about them a couple of years back—her late husband Otto was a collector."

"Well, I'm sure the Galaxes have a perfectly good explanation," Cam said.

"Which brings us to the second dilemma! Do we ask—which lets them know I went where I wasn't supposed to go?" Samantha said. "Or do we go straight to the police?"

"*Or do nothing,*" Tabby added.

Cam rubbed his hands together. "Let me think about it," he said. "In the meantime, can you send me your photos of the paintings?"

***

Freshwater Refurbishing on the bank of Lake Huron forty miles northeast of Rusted Bonnet looked nothing like the bustling port businesses Cam had seen in Baltimore and Norfolk. A short gravel track from a rutted road led to a single metal building the size of a McDonald's. From its side entrance, Cam could see a wooden rectangle jutting out into the lake—if pressed, he'd describe it as a floating dock rather than a pier.

Cam had tagged along to the shop with Becka and her girlfriend Missy, because, as Becka said, "I have no idea if people who work in the ship repair trade will talk straight to a couple of women." Missy had added that female empowerment took a back seat to $45,000.

Freshwater was Gak Blom's last—and only—place of employment in the States. Shortly after he died, Becka moved from the house they shared. She'd donated, recycled, or trashed most of his possessions save for a few keepsakes, none of which included 200 pounds of silver.

Becka didn't know of any friends her father had save for a co-worker from Freshwater named Dickie Fenwick. Unable to locate any contact information for Fenwick—whether by the name of Dickie or Richard—Missy had suggested a trip to the shipyard.

Cam pulled open a heavy outer door then an inner screen.

Becka and Missy followed him inside. Becka's lissome build contrasted with Missy's stocky frame. A man in a paint-speckled V-necked tee sat on a low chair, his knees spread wide. He appeared to be carving something with a knife. His yellow eyes looked up at them. "Y'all looking for an afternoon sail?" he asked, and before anyone could answer added, "We don't do those here. J. Dub's up a couple of blocks can fix ya' up though. He's my cousin."

"J. Dub's?" Becka repeated.

"Joseph Winchester's Ferry Excursions, but J. Dub's will do ya' just as good."

"We're not here for a pleasure cruise," Cam said. "You wouldn't happen to be Dickie Fenwick, would you?"

"Ha!" the man laughed and spat on the floor to one side. "Now do I look like a sunburned sloth to you?"

"No," Cam said slowly.

"That's for sure," he said. "Dickie, he's got these great big black sloth eyes with skin real pale-like and red-like, color depending on the light, of course. Not albino or Indian or nuthin' like that. Jus' sunburned sloth."

"Is he here?" Cam tried.

The man spat again to the side then scraped his knife against the wooden block in his other hand. "He'll be 'round 'bout seven o'clock tomorrow mornin'," he said. "His youngest had to git herself to the dentist and Dickie drew the short straw between he and the missus. But I'm owner here so if you're not lookin' for a cruise of sorts, what are ya'll looking for? We do topside maintenance, engine repair, and all the inspections—U.S. and Canada. Can handle pretty much any 'laker'—tugs, ferries, dinner boats, small barges. Got more space back there than ya'd think." He jerked his chin to one side. Behind him, in a cavernous open space, a houseboat was hoisted four feet off of the ground resting on a support system comprised of cinder blocks and wooden planks.

"We were actually inquiring after Gak Blom," Cam said. "This is his daughter." He nodded at Becka.

"Ah, I see the resemblance," the man said. "An' I don't mean 'cause of the color of your skin. Ya' have the same nose as Gak. Looks nicer on you than him." His thin lips stretched into a smile.

"Thank you," Becka said. "I'm curious, how did you find my father when you hired him?"

"He found me. Good timing, too. My welder had gone an' got hisself sent up for smoking something he shouldn't ha' been smoking. 'Least not in public. Gak must've found hisself some sort of list of repair shops here in the States 'cause he blasted out what looked like a pretty generic e-mail. But he attached some pictures of work he'd done. And he wasn't looking for much in the way of money. More just wanted to get hisself over here. The legal way 'an all. So, I e-mail back and says to him that if he figures out all the paperwork, 'an all I have to do is sign my name, I'll do it. Mind you, t'was conditioned on him being as good as he says he was. And he was. Man could weld a boat, thas' for sure."

The man stood and scratched his neck with the knife blade. "There sure are a lotta you for a social call."

"We were wondering if my dad left anything here," Becka said. She shoved her hands in the pockets of her butterscotch-colored coat. "Personal items."

"Wish you woulda' come 'round after he died," the man said. "I gotta shed 'round back. Me an' Dickie an' your daddy kept stuff in there. Quint now, too—he's my new welder."

"What kind of things?" Missy asked.

"Nothin' illegal if thas' what you're thinkin'. Stuff the wives don't want 'round the house. I got some rifles an' snowshoes an' my daddy's collection of old *Playboys*. Dickie's got an ATV parked in there."

"What kinds of things did Gak have?" Cam asked.

"Don't know to be honest with 'ya. He had a trunk. Some ratty lookin' African thing. No offense, ma'am."

"None taken," Becka said. "You never looked inside?"

"Nope. Not that I didn't try."

Becka cocked her head to one side. "He kept it locked?"

"Sure did. Powerful lock like nothin' I ever seen. Brand called Sobo. Couldn't get through it wit' my bolt cutters."

"What were you doing trying to break into his chest?" Cam asked.

The man looked daggers at him. "Man, back off me. You come 'round askin' questions and I ain't been nothin' but polite."

Cam put up his hands. "Sorry."

"I only tried to get in after Gak died. I was surprised none of the family showed up to git it."

"I didn't know he had anything here," Becka explained. "Honestly, I never thought about it. I probably should've sent you an invitation to the funeral, too. Or at least the viewing. Though we only had a few people from the neighborhood."

"Don't worry 'bout that," he said and snapped the blade of his knife into its handle. "When he didn't show up a few days in a row, Dickie went online, found Gak's obit."

"Is his trunk still here?" Cam asked.

The man shook his head. "Nope. Thing took up too much space. 'Course, I didn't git 'round to chuckin' it 'til a few months ago. Had to git J. Dub to help me carry the thing out to the curb. Thing weighed as much as a ton of bricks."

Chapter 10

"How's Richard?" Cam asked his mother. With Kacey working late, Cam had volunteered to watch Emma and invited Darby to his townhouse for taco night. Emma was tackling a word search at the dining room table while he diced onions in the kitchen.

Delicate laugh lines traced Darby's forehead. "We pressed pause," she said and edged around him to fill a stoneware mug with water from the sink.

She had been dating the retired radiologist for several months. Cam, who had met Richard half a dozen times, found him to be reserved but witty.

He opened his mouth to question her but thought better of it.

"And how are you doing with Kacey?" Darby whispered, her eyes on Emma. The first grader was still focused on her puzzle.

"We're doing really well," Cam said and knifed into a bell pepper. "It's platonic for now. But I'm not dating anyone and I don't think she is, either. We're getting along better than ever." He looked up and added, "Other than the fact that I'm technically a suspect in Samir Orucov's murder."

"What?" Darby shouted.

Emma leapt off of her chair and ran into the kitchen. "What's wrong, Grammy?"

"Nothing, sweetie." Darby touched a finger to Emma's cheek. "How's your word search coming along?"

"I'm almost done. Daddy, can I have peas for my vegetable?"

"Absolutely." Cam locked eyes with his daughter and smiled. Emma broke the gaze and scuttled back to the dining room. Once Emma was out of earshot, Cam lowered his voice and quickly brought Darby up to speed.

"And what are you doing about it?" she asked when he finished.

"I've spoken with everyone who works at Paul Bearer's. But I haven't gotten anywhere." He drizzled canola oil into a skillet.

"Have you looked for the stolen ruby?"

"I hadn't thought of that," Cam admitted. "I wouldn't know where to start."

Darby tapped a finger against her chin. "How about the funeral home itself?"

"Why would the robber leave it there?" Cam set a gas burner to medium heat and scraped the aromatics from his cutting board into the pan.

"Maybe he was afraid of the police searching his house and stashed the necklace until he could sell it."

Cam's mind sprang to the roofies stowed in the chocolate box. There certainly were plenty of places at Paul Bearer's one could hide a ruby.

***

After dinner, Cam drove Emma and a thermal pack nearly bursting with leftovers to Kacey's bungalow in the center of the village. He reheated and assembled tacos alongside red beans and rice while she tucked Emma into bed.

"Thanks, Cam," Kacey said, as he set a plate and a glass of Malbec in front of her. "For dinner and for watching Emma."

"It was my pleasure." He poured himself a glass of water. "I saw Ramón today."

"At Safeway?"

He nodded. "Before I knew Emma was coming for dinner, I had planned to make a green curry and needed a few items." He laughed. "I wanted to make Thai-style green beans as a side dish, but a woman in the produce aisle thwarted that."

"She took the last of the beans?"

"If only! No, she couldn't get the plastic produce bag open at first. So, she licked her fingers to help, then dipped the same hand into the bin to grab a handful of beans."

"Eww!"

"Exactly," Cam said. "But all is well with Ramón." Still standing, Cam sipped his water and set the glass on Kacey's inlaid Spanish tile table.

"What did you say?"

"That I 'noticed' he forgot to charge me for some produce the last few times I checked out. I said I hoped he'd be more careful because I didn't want any preferential treatment. He got the point."

"I'm glad," Kacey said, scooping a spoonful of rice and beans.

"Any interesting developments on Samir's murder since this morning?" Cam asked.

Kacey finished chewing her bite and swallowed. "I learned a couple of new things."

Cam parked himself at the table.

"But you're a suspect, Cam."

"Not a real one."

"Not to me," she said, "just Bernie, although you're pretty

low on his list at the moment." Kacey sipped her wine and appeared to be thinking. She took a second sip then said, "I heard back from the lab. A different knife was used on Markuss than the one we found in Samir. Samir was killed with a diving knife—one with a serrated titanium blade. Like the type a scuba diver would carry for emergencies. Forensics thinks Markuss was sliced with something slimmer, maybe a boning knife or something similar that you'd find in a kitchen."

"Do you have any idea what happened to it?"

"I don't have a clue." Kacey batted a strand of hair from the front of her face. "The main floor of Paul Bearer's doesn't have a kitchen, and the knife block in the apartment was full. Though Samir and Mitzy had a handful of other knives in a kitchen drawer, so it could've come from there."

"Is there any chance the killer wiped it clean and put it back?"

"It's possible."

"Did Mitzy know whether anything was missing?"

Kacey harrumphed. "She had no idea. I don't think she's cooked a meal in years. Mind you, she knew exactly how many corkscrews she owned."

Cam chuckled. He rose and drifted toward the refrigerator. "I brought a little dessert, too." He pulled open the freezer and extracted a carton of salted caramel ice cream from a well-stocked shelf.

"I bet Emma loved that." She exchanged a smile with Cam. "Did she ask for strawberry syrup?—she puts it on everything sweet these days."

"She asked, but I didn't have any at home. I'll make sure to get some the next time I'm at the store."

"You're doing a really good job with her," Kacey said and looked down at her plate.

"I'm just making up for lost time." Cam turned and reached

for a bowl in an overhead cabinet. "You said you learned a couple of new things in the case, right?"

Kacey picked her head up. "Yes, Shane gave me a fascinating alibi and the best laugh I've had in ages. When I asked him where he'd been on Monday night, he said—and I quote—'Oh, no, you're not making me the escape goat.'"

Cam snorted. "The only thing better than a misused cliché is unproper grammar."

Kacey burst into a laugh. She quickly clapped a hand over her mouth. "I hope I didn't wake Emma."

"So, what did Einstein have to say for himself?"

"That he went to the movies. But here's the weird thing—he went with *Markuss*."

Cam jammed a spoon into the half-gallon of ice cream and heaped a scoop into a bowl. He squeezed a dollop of Hershey's syrup onto its apex and set the offering in front of Kacey.

"Markuss and Shane went to the movies together," he repeated.

"That's what Shane said. And Markuss confirmed it. The latest Bond film at eight."

"At the theater in town?"

"Yes. Then they went for burgers."

"Markuss sure had himself a full night. He embalms Mr. Szubek, drives Jana to water aerobics, hits a movie and late dinner with Shane, and comes back to Paul Bearer's in time to get attacked. All during a snow storm." Cam stuffed the ice cream carton back in the well-stocked freezer.

"You're not having any?"

"I had a bowlful with Emma," he said. "I have a hard time picturing Markuss going to the movies with Shane. They're not exactly contemporaries. And when I saw him at the funeral home earlier that day, he made a crack about how dumb Shane is."

Kacey chewed on her lower lip. "Boxing *rings* are square—

some things just defy logic. But I sure wouldn't have pegged them as friends. That's why I thought it was so interesting."

"Was it just the two of them?"

Kacey furrowed her brow. "I didn't ask, but neither one suggested anyone had joined them."

Cam slapped a palm down on the table. "Markuss told me he went back to Paul Bearer's on Monday night because he forgot his wallet."

"So how could he have paid for his movie ticket," Kacey added, finishing his thought.

Cam rubbed an eyebrow with his thumb. "Shane could have paid."

"Or maybe Markuss keeps a few emergency dollars in his car. I do."

Cam dropped onto a chair. "When I visited Markuss in the hospital, I'm almost certain he said that he didn't even realize he'd left his wallet at Paul Bearer's until he was getting ready for bed. And he sure didn't mention the movies."

"You visited Markuss?"

"I did," Cam squeaked sheepishly. "Hey, I'm a suspect. I'm entitled to try to ferret out who attacked him."

"Entitled?" Kacey asked.

Cam grunted.

"It's possible he was having memory problems," she said letting him off of the hook, "especially if he was medicated when you spoke to him."

"Maybe. But something doesn't smell right."

Kacey brightened. "I agree."

"What about the others from Paul Bearer's? Do they all have alibis, too?"

"Mitzy admitted that she passed out in her closet—not exactly something we can corroborate, but it's believable enough. Piper said she was at home alone. She called a friend around eight o'clock. She still uses a landline so we were able to verify that it was in use for forty minutes. Of course, after she dialed the number, she could've hightailed it to Paul Bearer's and killed Samir before going home to hang up."

"But that suggests the friend on the other end of the line was involved."

"Perhaps," Kacey said. "But even if Piper contrived the call while stabbing Samir, it doesn't provide her cover for Markuss's attack. He told me that he returned to Paul Bearer's around eleven."

"So, they weren't attacked at the same time?"

"It doesn't look like it."

"Did you ask Markuss if he saw Samir's dead body?"

"He said he didn't, which makes sense if he parked in back and went straight to the prep room."

"But he wasn't attacked in the prep room."

"He told me he was, then he staggered into the hallway."

"Did you find a trail of blood?"

"No, but that's not surprising. With a wound like his, it probably took a minute or two to seep through his clothes."

"Do Blair and Jelly Roll have alibis?" Cam asked.

"Blair doesn't. She said she lit a fire at home, drank a half bottle of Pino Grigio, and watched the snow fall. Jelly Roll was helping a friend move."

"In a snow storm?"

"Apparently, the friend—a guy named 'Crater'—was starting a new job in Muskegon on Tuesday morning, and had to make the drive overnight. Jelly said he spent an hour and a half with Crater lugging furniture into a U-Haul."

"Crater, Jelly Roll, how do these guys get these names?"

Kacey licked her spoon. "Search me. I have an officer trying to find Mr. Crater. Jelly said he thought Shane agreed to go to the movies just to get out of hauling furniture with him."

"Laziness does seem to be right up Shane's alley. Is there any chance Piper and Blair were working together?"

"How so?"

"Maybe Piper called Blair. She's the person on the other end of the line and that gives Piper forty minutes to run to Paul Bearer's and off Samir. And she was the first person back in the morning. All Blair would have to do is keep the phone line open. Maybe Piper takes care of Samir at eight and Blair goes after Markuss at eleven."

"I don't think that's the case," Kacey said. "We tracked the number Piper called. It wasn't Blair. Looks like it was a woman in Toledo. For what it's worth, she confirmed that she and Piper spoke for forty minutes."

Chapter 11

The heavy night air clung to Cam's lungs like a mouthful of gluey risotto. At nine o'clock, he slipped into Paul Bearer's flower room—the door was unlocked.

Cam unlaced his boots and tiptoed stocking-footed into the hall, then spent thirty minutes in silence, searching every nook of the prep and storage rooms, chapel, great hall, and lounge for the missing ruby necklace. Only when he stepped from the lounge into the corridor near the stairs to the apartment, did he hear muffled voices coming from above.

Cam padded up the wooden steps. When he reached the door at the top, he crouched and pushed an ear against it. Two voices —one that sounded like Mitzy's and one, a man's—garbled through the wood. A minute later, an interior door slammed shut.

Cam tried the door handle. It twisted without resistance, but he hesitated instead of pushing it open. He could turn tail before getting caught—he *was* breaking and entering. He could tiptoe back downstairs and search the handful of rooms he hadn't yet inspected. Or, he could venture forth and see if he could glean who was with Mitzy behind door number one.

If it was Shane, that would make sense. So would a friend who was consoling her. *Who else might she be with at night in her apartment?*

Cam sucked in a sharp breath, cracked open the apartment door, and peeked through the gap. The dark front room offered no hint, so he pushed his way inside. On his hands and knees, his gray matter armed with a rough blueprint from jockeying a Dirt Devil about the space, Cam navigated around a sofa, past a curio cabinet, to a hallway that stretched to his left. At the end of the hall, a slash of light spouted from under a closed door— Mitzy's bedroom.

Cam crawled slowly toward the light. If Mitzy burst through the door, he'd have nowhere to hide. Five feet from it, the sound heard was unmistakable. Mitzy was *with* a man. *Three nights after her husband was murdered.*

Cam backed out of the apartment and ran down the stairs, shoved on his boots, then raced to his Chevy Malibu parked three blocks away. He cranked on the engine, pulled the car closer to the home, and killed the lights.

Other than the garage, Paul Bearer's had six exit doors. From his position, Cam could watch the front entry and three others, each lit by an outdoor sconce. He hunkered down and scanned the parking lot—save for the Orucovs' Lincoln and Cherokee, it was barren.

After fifteen minutes of still air, small bits of hail began to pepper the Malibu's windshield. Within minutes, it morphed into flurries then to fat flakes of snow. Cam flipped on the wipers and tuned the car radio to an AM news station. The broadcaster forecasted at least an inch overnight.

In desperate need of a caffeine-infused jolt, but not daring to leave his post, Cam settled for scrounging in the Malibu's center console, scoring a stale restaurant mint. Ten minutes later, the door near the lounge opened. A figure bound in a knee-length coat, scarf, and snow hat stepped outside. It looked like a man, but between the distance and snowfall, Cam couldn't make out his face. The figure briskly walked toward the parking lot—facing away from the Malibu. Cam leapt out of his car, donned heavy gloves, pulled a woolen cap around his ears, and started after him at a clip.

The figured crossed the parking lot to the street. Seconds later, a pickup truck sporting a garish spoiler beeped and its lights flashed. Cam made a split-second decision, spun on his heel, and darted back to the Malibu. He jumped inside and drove directly toward the pickup, his lights blazing. As Cam turned the corner, he caught a clear look at the face of the man brushing snow from the truck's windshield. Chet Szubek.

***

Cam dunked a buffalo drumstick into a bleu cheese bath. Traffic was light at the Stagger Inn for a Thursday night. Likely, a result of the snow.

He had positioned himself at a small table near the back of the bar where he could think in relative peace. Earlier in the week, Chet and Mitzy had both acted strangely at the mention of the other's name, suggesting to him this evening had not been their first foray into the physical. *Could Chet have killed Samir to pave the way for him and Mitzy to be together?*

The thought seemed farfetched. Mitzy was forty-six or forty-seven years old, even if she looked younger, and Chet in his mid-twenties. Cam could see Chet pursuing her for a bit of fun, but would he go so far as to *murder* Samir? Or could Mitzy have brainwashed him into it? Cam recalled a news story from years earlier—an older woman seducing a teenager, intent on having him shoot her husband. He sipped Pepsi and mentally added Chet Szubek to his catalog of suspects.

Discounting any alibis, his primary suspect list stood at six: Mitzy, Shane, Jelly Roll, Blair, Piper, and now Chet. Maybe seven, if he added Markuss despite his being attacked.

Cam crunched on a carrot stick. Mitzy had the strongest motive—she seemed fed up with Samir and her life in Rusted Bonnet. Selling the home amounted to a one-way ticket back to Baku. Shane, of course, thought that his mother would just turn over Paul Bearer's to him—and Jelly Roll by extension—after his father passed away. Cam couldn't put his finger on a concrete motive for Blair yet, but no one who kept illegal drugs in her handbag garnered a pass in his book. Kacey posited that Piper might be Markuss's daughter, and that Samir could've bilked the embalmer years earlier. And now there was Chet Szubek: former hometown hockey star and Mitzy's lover.

"Cam," a faint voice said.

He looked up. Blair's crystalline eyes adopted a tapioca hue under the glow of glazed light fixtures.

"S-sorry, Blair," he stuttered. "I didn't see you."

"I noticed." She sipped bubbles from a flute.

"Would you like to join me?"

"Certainly." She curled into the chair opposite him, tucking one foot underneath her backside.

"How's the champagne here?" Cam asked.

"It's supposed to be Prosecco, but it tastes more like soda water and Pop Rocks." She examined the liquid with a playful eye. "What are you drinking?"

"Just pop," Cam said, aware that he'd reverted from calling it "soda" since moving back to his hometown. "Though I think I'll switch to beer for the next one."

"I'll get it for you," Blair said and sprang to her feet. She seemed to exaggerate the sway of her hips as she approached the bar. *She's never shown such an interest in me before*, Cam thought.

A wall of denim cut Cam's view. Jelly Roll, standing behind the chair Blair had just vacated, was strangling a bag of Andy Capp's Hot Fries in one hand and shoving a fistful of the snack into his maw with the other.

Cam touched a forefinger to his forehead and flicked it toward Jelly Roll—a meathead salute.

The big man jerked his chin upward in response. "How are 'ya doing?" he said through a mouthful of chips. Orange stains marred his teeth.

"Just fine. And you?"

"Not too hot right now." He laughed and flecks of food fluttered down from his mouth to the seat of the chair. "I'll be doing better once Shane convinces his mom to stick around and keep the home."

"So that Shane can run it?"

"Shane and me. Plus, Miz Orucov is nice scenery."

Cam's mind flashed to Chet. *Was Mitzy into all younger men or just Chet?* "She's a single woman now," he said flatly.

Jelly Roll made a guttural sound. "Fat lot of good that'll do me. She doesn't think much of me."

I can't imagine why. Before Cam could respond out loud, Blair sidled back to the table.

"Get lost, Jelly," she said curtly. "Cam and I are having a drink."

The hearse driver grunted, jammed his hand inside the snack bag, and walked toward the bar.

Blair wordlessly brushed her seat with the back of a hand and slipped into it. She slid a draft in front of Cam and gave him a sugary smile, devouring him with her eyes.

"Thanks," he said nervously and sipped foam.

Chapter 12

A jackhammer pounded Cam's skull under hair matted with sweat. He cracked open heavy eyelids and squinted down at the blanket covering his body—the John Deere green one his grandmother had quilted for him as a teenager. He twisted his neck toward the nightstand clock: 11:26 a.m. Cam hadn't slept past eight o'clock in years. He rubbed crust from his eyes and peeked under the blanket at his shirtless torso. He never slept without a tee shirt.

Had the gluten in the beer knocked him out? No, he thought —beer was an exception he allowed himself, and while it often upset his stomach, he'd never felt like this before.

Had he spent the night with someone? Cam lifted his head, no easy effort with a steel drum beating its insides, and scanned the room. No sign of a woman. Then the prior night's events blasted back to him in a torrent—Blair Lamb shoveling compliments in his direction over drinks. And then his recollection was completely blank. The last thing Cam remembered was finishing his third beer as Blair twirled her hair and checked her watch. *Did she bring me home?* Cam felt both self-satisfied and guilty. But why should he be? He and Kacey weren't together.

Cam wrenched himself upright. The feeling of tiny drills dug into his back and legs. His clothes from the previous night were folded neatly on his dresser, save for his Calvin Klein boxer briefs, which were still on. *Had he and Blair even done anything?*

Two minutes later, Cam found the energy to wobble into the shower. Relishing the heat and feeling smug, he allowed scalding water to pelt his chest. Then another thought twisted into his aching head. He'd never blacked out after three drinks before in his life. *Blair must have slipped Rohypnol into his beer.*

***

"Drugged?" Kacey shouted from the other end of the phone. A mechanical screech drowned out her voice.

"Yes!" Cam yelled back. "I can't hear you! Where are you?" He had called Kacey as soon as he finished showering and forced down three ibuprofen and a bowl of hot tomato soup.

Cam could barely hear her say, "At Paul Bearer's," over the sound of grinding gears.

The quaking in his head had dulled to a four on the Richter scale by the time he reached the funeral home. A half dozen black-and-whites and three television vans, one with a mini satellite dish attached to its roof, crowded the corner of the parking lot nearest the octagonal-shaped lounge.

Swarms of people gathered on the pavement in front of Paul Bearer's. The snow hadn't been plowed and Cam sloshed through powder melting under a penetrating sun. A menacing looking wrecking crane arched toward the sky, hovering over the lounge. Just in front of the funeral home's main entrance, two men in canary yellow hard hats stood as part of a circle with Kacey, Chief Leftwich, Mitzy, and a stocky man with a bulbous nose in a dark overcoat. The conversation looked heated, although Mitzy—who was wearing a wool skirt and no stockings—was shivering.

To one side of the circle, news reporters and their camera crews stood at the ready.

Cam spotted a familiar journalist standing alone. Geoffrey Rampart, a columnist with the *Rusted Bonnet Observer,* had been Cam's tenth grade English teacher. According to Samantha, who seemed to know every villager's secrets, Geoffrey had lied on his resume. The falsehood first came to light after twenty years on the job. He was in line for a promotion to vice principal and the school district ran a background check—something that hadn't been the practice when he was hired. Apparently, Mr. Rampart claimed to have dual degrees in English literature and linguistics, rather than one in anthropology. After the school ousted Geoffrey to 'set an example,' he spent eighteen months as a copy editor in the basement of the village paper's office before being offered the opportunity to write.

"Hi, Geoffrey," Cam said as he approached. "What's happening here?"

The older man brightened. "Cam, good to see you. There's some sort of stand-off between Mitzy Orucov and this demolition crew."

"Someone's trying to knock down the funeral home?"

"It sure looks that way. One of the cameramen from Channel Two told me he heard it's going to become a strip mall."

Cam, his head still smarting, felt like a boxer who had taken a hard uppercut to the chin. "A strip mall?" he repeated. "I can't believe Mitzy sold the property so quickly."

"I don't think this was her doing," Geoffrey said. "When I arrived, she was standing in front of the octagon there with her arms outstretched like a hippie trying to save a tree."

***

Five minutes later, Mitzy stormed into the funeral home, slamming the door behind her, and the rest of her circle dispersed. The stocky man lowered himself into a large Audi and drove off. One of the hard-hatted men climbed into the driver's seat of the crane and backed it away from Paul Bearer's. Bernie made a short statement to the media: "There's a dispute over the ownership of the funeral home, which will need to be worked out through our legal system."

Cam caught Kacey's eye as she turned toward her cruiser. He lobbed a quick good-bye in Geoffrey's direction and caught up with her.

"Can we get a cup of coffee? I really need to talk with you."

She jerked up her wrist to check her watch, seemingly flustered. "Are you all right?" she asked and marched to her car. "It was hard to hear you on the phone over the crane. Do you really think you were drugged?"

Cam followed, shielding the sun from his eyes. "Yes, I think Blair Lamb slipped something in my drink last night at the Stagger."

Kacey stopped abruptly and spun to face him. "That's a major accusation." Her breath was visible in the bitter air. "You'll have to make a formal statement down at the station if you're serious."

"Unfortunately, I am."

Kacey's eyes warmed. "Why don't I drive you."

When they reached the police car, Cam slid into the passenger's seat.

"Are you all right?" Kacey asked and started the engine.

"I think so. It hasn't all sunk in yet." He recounted as much as he could remember as they drove.

"So you didn't actually see her put anything into your drink?" Kacey asked when he finished.

"No. But she could have at the bar. I saw the roofies in her purse the night before."

"And you don't know if you were, um, taken advantage of?"

He stared straight ahead. "No."

"Cam, was anything taken from your house?"

"Taken?"

Kacey braked and Cam's crown slammed back into the headrest. The ache in his grey matter sharpened. "I didn't look," he said. "Stealing never even crossed my mind, but that would make sense. I couldn't imagine why a woman as attractive as Blair would knock me out. Can we go to my place first so I can look around?"

"Sure," Kacey said and changed her driving course. "I'll need to call the chief when we get there and tell him there's a situation warranting my immediate attention."

"So, what was with the hard hat convention?" Cam asked.

"For me, a lesson in learning not to jump to conclusions." Kacey squawked like a bird. "I assumed that Samir left the funeral home to his wife."

"He left it to Shane?" Cam asked.

"Apparently, neither. At least according to Mr. Jackson de Winter, the third."

"Was he the short man in the overcoat?"

"And expensive-looking tie and shoes. He hired the demo crew to tear down the home. Thankfully, they had the good sense to make sure no one was in the building before they got started. Mitzy was inside."

"Just her?" Cam asked.

Kacey shot him a sideways glance. "Who else would be in there? She hasn't reopened yet."

Chet Szubek back for more? Cam wanted to say, but he didn't think Kacey or the chief would take kindly to his breaking into Paul Bearer's. "No one. Samir left Mr. de Winter the funeral home?"

"Not exactly. According to Mitzy, the will bequeaths all of Samir's possessions to her. But de Winter claims that he already owned Paul Bearer's."

Cam raised an eyebrow. "So, the property would fall outside of the will."

"Exactly. According to de Winter, he bought the place a year-and-a-half ago. Samir was leasing it back."

"But Mitzy didn't know?"

"Precisely. She said she had no idea and claimed that Jackson de Winter is full of ... you know. She actually spat on his shoes."

Cam chuckled. "Sounds like her. So now what?"

"The chief told de Winter to stand down until there's a court order one way or another. So, I imagine a bunch of lawyers will swoop down."

"What's a group of lawyers called—a quarrel?"

"Funny," Kacey said, but didn't laugh.

"Have you seen de Winter before? I mean, if he's a legitimate businessman I can't imagine he'd try to knock down a building he didn't own."

"I haven't and neither had Bernie. But he said he's a commercial real estate investor and owns a dozen properties in metro Detroit, so he should turn up easily enough in a records search."

"Do you care? Now that the impasse is over, I mean."

"I only care if Jackson de Winter stabbed Samir in the back." She jackknifed the cruiser into a spot in front of Cam's townhouse between a beaten-up Volvo and an oversized SUV.

"Jackson de Winter is a suspect?"

"Why not?" Kacey jerked the transmission into park.

"What would he stand to gain by killing Samir? If he owns Paul Bearer's, he could've just kicked him out."

"Maybe Samir had a long-term lease and de Winter decided he wanted to shorten it." Kacey popped open the car door. "No, that's weak." She turned to Cam. "I don't know why he'd want to kill Samir, but anyone who tries to knock down a man's building less than a week after he's murdered warrants a close look."

***

"Amazing," Cam said after rummaging through his townhome for thirty minutes. He couldn't find a single thing missing. Not the rainy-day twenties flattened between two icepacks in the freezer or the pair of emergency hundreds rolled into a travel toothbrush case in the master bath. Not the Movado watch his mother had given him as a college graduation present or the tarnished silver he and Kacey had registered for—and used a grand total of one time. Not his smart phone, tablet, or the LCD television on the living room wall.

"Do you keep credit card statements anywhere?" Kacey asked. She was bent over a low bench near Cam's front door re-lacing her shoes. "Maybe she copied down the numbers?"

"No," Cam said. "I get them electronically now. Bank statements, too. And I shred anything that happens to come in the mail." He snapped his fingers and dug a hand into his back pocket. "I never checked my wallet." He quickly rifled through its contents. "Everything's here. Of course, she could've copied down my credit card numbers. I better call to check if they've been used."

Kacey uprighted herself and placed a hand on the doorknob. "Let me know if there are any charges that look amiss. Do you still want to make a statement?"

Cam ran a hand over his face. "Do you think I should?"

Kacey took a step closer to Cam and laid a hand on his chest. "I do. With a formal statement, I can convince a magistrate to issue a search warrant. With that, I can seize any pills that are in Blair's purse. It's a good start."

Chapter 13

Windsor, Ontario, had the dubious distinction of being the reining smog capital of Canada. Located downwind of Detroit, coal-fired Motown power plants pumped pollutants across the river into the city.

At eight o'clock on Friday night, Cam's Malibu idled at the back of a line for border customs stretching an eighth of a mile. With a drinking age of nineteen in Ontario, a steady stream of vehicles stuffed with college freshmen and sophomores flooded east over the Ambassador Bridge or through the Detroit-Windsor tunnel into Canada every weekend. Most would make a beeline for The Honest Lawyer, Bar-Bar-Black Sheep, and a bevy of other hotspots along Chatham Street and Ouellette Avenue.

Gannon Galax had retired from his position as a professor of visual arts at the University of Windsor five years earlier. A simple Internet search on Gannon and his wife Kamila yielded that snippet of information, along with the fact that Kamila had served on the board of trustees at the Predmore—the most notable gallery in the Windsor environs. Art experts with three pricy pieces squirreled forty miles away—and in another country no less—spurred Cam's curiosity. *The Galaxes could be investors*, he thought, but they also could know enough to be thieves. Yet, Cam hadn't found any reports online about stolen or missing paintings by Denys Rouland.

The Predmore's website touted a black tie fundraiser that evening; RSVPs for the soiree were preferred but tickets could be purchased at the door. Cam doubted that scavenging for scuttlebutt on Gannon and Kamila would be worth the $100 "donation," but impulse urged him to flee Rusted Bonnet for the night, especially after making a gut-wrenching statement at the police station about being drugged. It was better than holing up under his blankets.

After crawling through customs, wearing his late father's hand-me-down tuxedo, spruced up with a new charcoal necktie, Cam entered a sea of Ontario's upper crust. Black-and-white-garbed waitstaff passed trays of crab canapés, prosciutto-wrapped mozzarella, and beef carpaccio atop parmesan crisps. A pair of bars enjoyed lines ten-people deep. But Cam had no taste for alcohol after his experience the previous night.

The crowd appeared to sway collectively like a sailboat adrift in a light wind. According to the Predmore's website, Ronald Tremblay chaired its board as well as the university's visual arts department. But Cam hadn't seen a photograph of him online, so had no idea what the man looked like. Presumably others at the soirée would know Gannon or Kamila, perhaps even both of them, but Tremblay was the only name he knew.

The gallery's visual offerings ran the gamut: lavish oils in gilded frames hung juxtaposed to frameless modern photographs. A gaggle of women, clad in floor-length gowns, fawned over a beach scene watercolor. Cam wove through the assemblage to a smaller room jutting off of the gallery's west end. A simple poster board standing on a tripod was emblazoned with the words, "Silent Auction."

Cam stepped into the auction area. Fifteen paintings, give or take a couple, stood on easels around three sides of the room. Two large sculptures—nudes—and a small table bearing ceramic pots splashed with vibrant purples and aquas commanded the center of the room.

A numbered index card marked with a dollar minimum sullied the environs of each piece, and a table at the back of the room held small boxes for bidding slips. Cam scanned the cards as he meandered—the least expensive of the bunch was almost an order of magnitude higher than the balance in his checking account.

"Magnificent, isn't it?" Cam heard as he stood admiring a pastel on canvass capturing a winter park-scape. He glanced over his shoulder at the speaker, then turned toward her.

"It is," he said. "Though I have to admit I'm not familiar with this artist."

"He's a gem," the woman said. Her hair was the color of spun cotton, her eyebrows, ribbons of a deep blue-gray.

"Are all of his works winter scenes?" Cam asked.

The woman sipped from a champagne flute. "No. In fact, this is the first of his I've seen with snow. Are you planning to bid on it?"

Cam glanced at the index card resting on the easel—an $18,000 minimum. "Unfortunately, it's a bit out of my price range at present."

"And I expect it'll go for closer to twenty-five. Most of Agnusdei's works do. I'm Valerie Plum by the way." She extended a hand.

Cam shook it lightly and introduced himself. Valerie's skeletal fingers contrasted with the baby fat in her cheeks.

"I haven't seen you here before," Valerie said.

"Tonight is the first chance I've had to see the gallery." Cam took a shallow breath, then added, "Gannon and Kamila Galax suggested I come."

Valerie smiled broadly, showing a quarter of an inch of gums. "You know Kamila! How is the dear?"

"She's doing very well," Cam bluffed. He'd only spoken with Kamila once since taking over at Peachy Kleen, and that was on the telephone. "She lives in Michigan now, an hour north of Detroit."

"Is that so? I knew she moved a few years back. Kamila was on the board here at the gallery."

"Did you know her well?"

"Just to have a small chat every now and again. She was always so lovely. I think she was married to an art history professor."

"Visual arts," Cam said with the confidence of a confidant. "At the university here in town."

"I see." She looked past Cam toward the pastel. "I think I may just put in a bid on this piece. Give Kamila my best, please." Valerie turned and took a step toward the bidding boxes.

"Ms. Plum?" Cam ventured before she was out of earshot.

She stopped and turned. "Mrs. Plum, please."

"You wouldn't happen to know Ronald Tremblay, would you?"

The older woman's eyes danced. "I most certainly do. He's my nephew."

***

Sandpaper skin and puckered dimples soured Ronald Tremblay's square jawline. Valerie and Cam found him tucking into a plate of peeled shrimp.

"I didn't see those, Ronnie," Valerie remarked by way of introduction.

Ronald wiped cocktail sauce from his upper lip with a napkin. "They're in the back, near the quartet."

"I may have to try one," she said. "Ronnie, this is Cam Reddick from Michigan. He knows Kamila Galax and her husband."

Cam reached out a hand and Ronnie shook it with a rough grip. "How are the old whipsaws?"

"Very good," Cam said. "They're neighbors of mine." He didn't dare tell Ronnie that he ran a housekeeping business, afraid of the reaction that might engender from the board chair.

"Good folks," Ronnie said. "I hated to see them go. Gannon was a professor in my department at the U."

"Visual arts, right?"

"Yes, sir. The man had one heck of a keen eye."

"Was he interested in paintings?" Cam asked.

Valerie, who had been ogling Ronnie's plate of shrimp, touched Cam on the forearm and excused herself.

"Paintings?" Ronnie repeated and set his plate on the tray of a passing waiter. "Sure. He taught photography, but he never met a medium he didn't like. Oils, clay, Gouache, you name it. Why do you ask?"

"I have a couple of originals by French painters," Cam fibbed. "They caught Gannon's attention."

"I have no doubt. I imagine Kamila would've been captivated, too, if they're any good. She was on the board here."

"I know. She's the one who told me about the function tonight," Cam lied.

"So, she does get the flyers we send!" He coughed then slammed a fist against his chest. "Mind if I get a drink?"

"I'll join you," Cam said, not wanting to lose him. He took a step toward the bar.

"No need to go anywhere," Ronnie said. He made eye contact with a model-thin woman standing near the front door of the gallery. She walked confidently toward the pair, her deep-set, raccoon eyes boring into Cam's. When she reached them, Ronnie whispered something into her ear and she swiveled and strode to the back of room and through a closed door.

"I hope you like bourbon," Ronnie said. "That's one perk of being the chair here—I don't wait in line for a drink. So, who do you have?"

Cam creased his eyebrows. "Who do I have?" he repeated.

"Which French painters?" Ronnie asked more sharply.

Before Cam could respond, the toothpick-framed woman returned and silently handed Ronnie and Cam tumblers filled to the brim. A bouquet of vanilla and toasted caramel assaulted his nostrils.

Ronnie lowered the lids on his washed-out eyes and breathed in heavily. "I never tire of this smell." He knocked back half of his drink in a single swallow and peered at Cam.

Cam took a small sip. Bourbon flames licked the back of his throat. "Very nice," he managed weakly.

"A man's drink for sure."

Cam nodded his head, then managed to squeak out, "Denys Rouland."

"Your originals are Roulands?" Ronnie cast a less-than-surreptitious glance at Cam's cheap duds.

"Yes," Cam answered with more bravado than he felt. "Do you have any here?" He pictured the chair answering: 'Not anymore; we had three go missing.'

Instead, he said, "Unfortunately not." Ronnie polished off his drink. "As far as I know, Captain Sickleson and his wife have the only Roulands in Windsor."

"Are they here this evening?"

Ronnie's eyes swept around the gallery. "I haven't seen them. The Captain is partial to the casino."

"Do you know which Roulands they have?"

Ronnie smoothed his fingers over a non-existent moustache. "I've never actually seen them. Kamila's the one who told me a few years back. I think she used to house sit for the Sickelsons when they went on vacation."

Saturday, February 13

Cam pored over Samantha's photos of the Roulands at his complimentary Holiday Inn Express breakfast—black coffee and rubbery hotcakes with sickeningly sweet syrup. Two of the paintings depicted pastoral scenes: one, a vast field of blooming sunflowers and the other, a tree-canopied stream. The third was more modern—stacks of crushed cars mottled with dull shades of pink—but with stylistic elements suggestive of the same artist.

A simple search on his phone between bites of pancake pinpointed the Sickleson's address. "Captain" Jasper and his wife Mimi—the only Sicklesons in the Windsor white pages—lived in the Lakeshore neighborhood, which, according to Google Maps, skirted the southern edge of Lake St. Clair to the east of Windsor.

At ten o'clock in the morning, dressed in a newly purchased wool sport coat and tie from Moores Clothing for Men—an addition he needed anyway—Cam turned his Malibu down the Sickleson's quarter-mile driveway. He jammed the car into park behind a boxy azure Bentley.

The red and white brick Georgian boasted three stories and four chimneys. Cam mounted wide stone steps onto a pillared porch replete with ceramic cherubs.

Cam rapped a brass knocker against a cherry-stained door. A young woman with flan-colored skin in low-slung jeans and a faded hoodie answered. "Can I help you?"

"I'm looking for Mr. or Mrs. Sickleson," Cam said, and bit his lower lip, willing his eyes to keep from dipping down to the woman's hips.

"Those would be my parents. I'll go get them." The woman bounded away, but called back over her shoulder: "My father goes by 'Captain,' not 'Mister.'"

Thirty seconds later, a couple, who looked as if they were turned out for dressage, approached the door together. "My daughter says you're looking for us," the man stated.

"Yes, sir." Cam bowed his head slightly. "My firm is working with Caesars Windsor," he said in a skittish voice— chum for a lie detector. "The casino is putting in an art gallery, similar to the one at the Bellagio in Las Vegas. Well, a bit smaller, of course."

"That's wonderful," gushed the woman. "I'm Mimi." She extended a plump hand. "Won't you please come in!"

Cam shook Mimi's hand, then the Captain's and introduced himself, using his real name. He followed them into a formal living room.

"Would you like tea?" Mimi asked, hovering above Cam as he sat on the edge of a leather chesterfield.

"No, thank you, ma'am," he said.

Mimi took a single step backward, but remained standing, close enough for Cam to smell a perfume redolent of freesia. A crystal vase of stargazer lilies adorned the glass coffee table between Cam and the Captain, who had wedged himself into an upholstered wingback. "So, what can *we* do for you?" the Captain asked. His canines were as sharp as a dromedary camel's.

Cam's jaw tightened. "I attended a fundraiser at the

Predmore last night…"

Mimi whinnied. She leveled her eyes in her husband's direction, then squatted beside Cam. "We were *supposed* to attend as well, but my dear Jasper couldn't drag himself away from the blackjack table." She softened her eyes, then added, looking at Cam, "Not that I don't enjoy your casino myself."

"I don't actually work at the casino,'" Cam said.

"Well, you know what I mean." Mimi rose.

A honeyed voice said, "Casinos and artwork: you've definitely come to the right house." Cam looked past Mimi. The woman who answered the door had donned form-fitting running pants. "I'm going for a jog, mom," she said and swept out the front door.

"Our daughter, Ashlie, home for a break from grad school," Mimi explained.

"Now, what does your work have to do with us, on a Saturday?" the Captain asked.

"Don't be so direct, Jasper," Mimi snapped. "How was the function last night?" she asked Cam and rested a hip against an arm of the chesterfield.

"It was splendid," he said, then focused on Jasper. "Sir, I'm trying to inventory the assets of local art patrons who have their own collections and might be interested in loaning the casino a piece or two until it can fill out the gallery. Mr. Tremblay told me you have a number of Roulands."

Jasper nodded, his Silly Putty chin bobbing. "We have three. How long would the gallery want them?"

"No more than twelve months," Cam said. *Three.*

"Will Caesars insure them?"

"Absolutely." He was anxious to see a Rouland up close.

Mimi didn't disappoint him. "Let me show them to you," she said. Her knees cracked as she straightened up. "We have oils by several Dutch artists, too. Might you be interested in those?"

"Perhaps," Cam said, springing to his feet. "But I wouldn't want your walls to be barren."

"Too true," the Captain agreed and wriggled free from the constricting bonds of the wingback.

Cam followed the pair through a marble foyer and a stainless-steel fortress that doubled as a kitchen to the dining room. Behind one head of an exquisite sandalwood table, under a thin track of brass lights, hung Rouland's sunflowers.

Cam's mouth went slack. It looked identical to one of the paintings secreted away in the Galax's attic. At least according to Samantha's photos.

"She's a beauty," the Captain remarked.

"Y-yes," Cam spluttered. "He did one other sunflower piece, I believe. It looked quite similar."

One of Jasper's eyes twitched. "Is that so? I thought ours was the only one."

Cam shivered.

Mimi took Cam by the arm and shuttled him into a great room. "The other two are in here," she said.

Cam stopped in the middle of the room, his knees locking. To the right of a bay window hung the tree-canopied stream in a gilt frame and above the fireplace, Rouland's flattened pink cars, stacked like rows of griddle cakes in a warming tray at the Holiday Inn's breakfast buffet.

Chapter 14

"I need help," Cam said, a crossword in hand as his mother dropped down across from him into a vinyl-backed booth at the Bear Claw.

"Anything." Darby set Tory Burch sunglasses on the table.

He pointed at the puzzle. "What's another word for synonym?"

She laughed.

Over blue-plate lunch specials, Cam relayed a litany of recent events to his mother, save for the blackout incident. He didn't want to worry her.

"I'm pretty certain that Chet left town," Darby said.

Cam swallowed chipped beef 'without the gravy.' "How do you know?"

"I stopped by Paul Bearer's yesterday. I had wanted to find out when Samir's funeral was being held."

"You're going?"

"No." Darby smiled and sipped iced tea through a straw. "But only because there isn't one. Don't forget, Samir was a client of mine for years. The police released his body yesterday and Mitzy had him cremated this morning."

"Cremated?"

"She said he was a rotten S.O.B. and was lucky she didn't just throw his body in the lake."

"I guess Samir really did sell Paul Bearer's under her feet."

"She said she didn't know what he did. She hired a lawyer, but said she wanted to confront de Winter herself, too."

"She could've taken Chet for a physical presence."

Darby smiled. "If she needs beef, she has Shane and Jelly Roll."

"How did you find out that Chet left town?" Cam nibbled on toasted crust.

"He was driving away at the same time I pulled in. Mitzy made an offhand comment. Something like, 'I imagine I won't see that one for another ten years.'"

"What do you think she meant?" Cam asked.

"I have no idea."

"You never heard rumors?"

"About Samir and Chet's mother...." Darby trailed off.

That was not the rumor Cam expected. He lowered his voice. "Samir was sleeping with Chet's mom?"

"I can't be certain," Darby said. "But a few years back— probably when Chet was in high school—I saw Chet's mother Steffi sneak into Paul Bearer's though the flower room door. Mitzy was out and I happened to be cleaning the place—either Samir didn't realize I was on the schedule that day or didn't care. And I had the unenviable task of cleaning the apartment at Paul Bearer's after she left an hour later. The bed reeked of sex."

"You can tell?" Cam asked.

"You can't?"

Cam shrugged. "Do you know if Mitzy found out?"

"I have no idea," Darby said. A waitress refilled her glass

with iced tea.

"I wonder…" Cam said—his turn to trail off.

Darby looked him in the eye. "Out with it."

"I heard Mitzy and Chet in bed together on Thursday night."

"What a family!" Darby rolled her eyes. "How did you manage to hear?"

"I was following your suggestion," Cam said, "looking for the ruby."

"Did you find it?"

Cam shook his head and chewed a bite of his lunch.

"Did you tell Kacey about Mitzy and Chet?"

He swallowed. "No, I think just going inside was illegal."

Darby snorted. "You're in there all of the time and you didn't take anything. I wouldn't worry about that."

"You forget that I'm a suspect," Cam said.

"And why would any suspect in his right mind go back to the crime scene?"

"To get rid of some evidence he left behind?" Cam guessed.

"Maybe, but getting it on with a widow just days after her husband dies seems higher on the suspicion meter to me."

"Suspicion meter?"

"Lust is always a motive for murder, isn't it?"

"On TV, I suppose," Cam said. "Though I don't think Chet needed to kill Samir to get into Mitzy's pants." He explained that he thought the pair may have had prior dalliances.

Darby sipped her drink. "I wonder if Mitzy seduced Chet *because* she found out that her husband had been with his mother."

"Sexual revenge?"

"Steffi Szubek has her way with Mitzy's man so she returns the favor."

"Why her son and not her husband?"

"You obviously haven't seen her husband. Chet didn't get his looks from him, that's for sure. Plus, as you know, Mitzy likes younger men."

As if on cue, the door to the Bear Claw flew open and Mitzy strode inside. She stomped snow from deerskin-colored UGGs onto the mat. Shane followed, dragging his feet in heavy work boots and leaving a trail of slush in his wake.

Mitzy's eyes sizzled when she spotted Cam, who was facing the door. She approached and exchanged greetings with him and Darby. Shane remained a step behind his mother.

"Cam, I saw you during my *altercation*," Mitzy said.

"I'm glad you were able to stop the crane," he said, brushing past why he had been at Paul Bearer's. He preferred no one know he was looking for Kacey because he thought he'd been drugged.

"For now." Mitzy swept a hand with dramatic flair across her brow and flipped fingertips into the air—a flourish more befitting Russet Bonnet High than Broadway. "That man is a vulture."

"Jackson de Winter?" Cam asked.

"The *third*," Mitzy breathed. "I think he will never let anyone forget that." She twisted her neck and said to Shane, "Get us a table and order me a cup of cottage cheese and a bowl of melon, please."

Shane shuffled off. Mitzy turned back to Cam. "Would you have a couple of free hours?"

"Right now?" Cam looked at his half-eaten lunch.

"After you finish, of course. I have an appointment to speak with Mr. *the third*." She blew a wisp of hair from her eyes. "Shane can loom like a ghoul, but he is not good for much else. I would like a brain in the room with me."

"Not your lawyer?"

"He will tell me to stay quiet. I do not want to stay quiet."

Cam glanced at his mother. She shrugged her shoulders.

"Sure, I can manage that," he said to Mitzy, secretly thrilled to have the chance to speak with de Winter.

She clapped her hands together. "Wonderful. Everyone in town knows you solved that murder last year. You have a good head on your shoulders. And a sexy one at that."

Darby cleared her throat.

"Oh, dear, even you know your son is a looker."

***

The glass-fronted building housing Jackson de Winter's twelfth-floor office suite in Detroit was shaped more like a cookie jar than a skyscraper. Nestled among a pocket of coffee shops and upscale eateries enveloped by burned out factories and abandoned tenements, the building's environs hyperbolized a Motor City makeover.

A woman with breasts distending a brassy lime top flitted around a reception desk to meet Mitzy, Cam, and Shane.

Shane leered at her bare navel. Mitzy wrinkled her nose, as if the woman's midriff was a child's sticky fingerprint on a freshly cleaned windowpane. Apparently, Mitzy—who wore comparably skimpy outfits at Paul Bearer's—raised her expectations of formality in an office.

"I have an appointment with Mr. de Winter," she said brusquely.

"You must be Ms. Orucov," the woman said and pulled at her short skirt. "Come right this way, please. He's expecting you." She led the trio down a short hall, past a small conference room and a brick of cubicles to a spacious office. An enormous metallic symbol of the Jedi Order emblazoned otherwise stark walls.

Jackson de Winter rose from behind a desk. "Gracias, Trix," he said and opened his arms in a welcoming gesture towards

Mitzy. "Thank you for coming on a Saturday. Won't you please sit down."

Mitzy looked at Shane and said, "You wait up front with *Trix*."

"Yes ma'am," he replied with an eager tone. Shane's boots managed to drip slush on the carpet—*he's like a leaky snow cone maker,* Cam thought. The pair departed and Mitzy introduced Cam.

He and Mitzy parked in sleek, armless chairs opposite de Winter. The man embodied a living, breathing geometry quiz— an egg-shaped forehead, isosceles chin, ninety-degree shoulders, and a perfect inverted triangle of white dress shirt from his Adam's apple down to the top button of his suit jacket.

de Winter lowered himself into a swivel chair and lifted a thin black binder. He extended it toward Mitzy, but his arms were too short to reach across the desk. Cam stood and accepted the binder. He handed it to Mitzy, who flipped it open.

"You'll find complete records of the sales transaction, including the deed," de Winter said with a trace of smugness.

Mitzy dug out a pair of wire-rimmed glasses from her satchel, an accouterment Cam had never seen her wear before.

"You're free to keep that copy," de Winter told Mitzy. "The upshot is that nineteen months ago, I bought Paul Bearer & Sons, both the building and the property it stands on. I paid $1.6 million dollars. One point one went to Flagstar to pay off the primary mortgage and the other five hundred thousand for the equity covered by the reverse mortgage."

Mitzy jerked her head upright. "Reverse mortgage?" she asked sharply. Her cheeks flamed red. "What the hell is that?"

A car salesman's grin stretched across de Winter's lips. "It's when a homeowner takes the equity he has and uses it to receive cash payments. Samir built up a half million in equity over the years and he was taking out money against that. From

Comerica. Of course, he was still paying on the remainder of the mortgage to Flagstar."

"The $1.1 million?" Cam asked.

"Yes," de Winter said. "Samir told me Paul Bearer's revenue wasn't enough to cover the mortgage and his bills. The reverse mortgage from Comerica supplied him with monthly cash infusions."

"I don't get it," Mitzy said. "Why would Comerica pay him?"

"Simple. Once the payments, along with a little interest for the bank themselves, exhausted the half million in equity, the bank would own that equity."

"So, Samir was using the reverse mortgage payments to turn around and pay the regular mortgage?" Cam asked.

"I can't be certain, but I believe so." de Winter poured himself a glass of water from a carafe. "Then Samir could use the money he made at Paul Bearer's to pay his regular monthly bills."

"But at the end of the day, he wouldn't have any equity in the home, right?" Cam said. "The whole thing would be owned by the two banks."

"Correct."

"Wait!" Mitzy jumped to her feet. "Samir, that mother … you-know-what, planned to leave me a stupid funeral home worth zero?"

"Worth nothing to you," de Winter said. "It would still be worth $1.6 million, just to the banks."

Mitzy growled. "For years, Samir makes the mortgage payments and has money 'a plenty for bills and everything else. What changed? Business was not bad. When did he take out this —this reverse mortgage thing?"

"Five years ago. I don't know what changed in his business practices."

"Hold on," Cam said. "He'd built up a half million of equity, then five years ago he started cutting into that. But he only sold the property to *you* nineteen months ago, right?"

de Winter nodded.

"I can't imagine in the three years and five months between taking out the reverse mortgage and selling to you, Comerica paid out five hundred grand, even with their interest. Samir must have gotten a lump sum from you."

Mitzy shot Cam a hopeful look.

"You're quite astute," de Winter said and sipped his water. "But there's a wrinkle."

"Let us hear it," Mitzy grumbled, finally sitting back down.

"Under the scenario as Mr. ... Reddick was it? described it, the money would have flowed like this: I paid $1.6 million for the funeral home and the land it sits on. Approximately $1.1 million went to Flagstar—the bank with the primary mortgage. Approximately $150,000 went to Comerica to buy out the reverse mortgage. Leaving a lump of $350,000."

"So even if you have the deed, Samir was still worth three-fifty," Mitzy said then took a deep breath. "That should come to me through the will."

de Winter blinked several times. "That's where the wrinkle comes in."

Mitzy's neck muscles bulged.

"There are restrictions on a reverse mortgage," de Winter explained. "Certain legal regulations apply to the issuing banks. First, they're designed for homes, not commercial property. I suppose Samir convinced Comerica that the funeral home qualified because of the apartment upstairs."

"We have *lived* there for almost thirty years," Mitzy said.

"Of course," de Winter allowed, not sounding like he cared one way or the other. "The other main limitation is there's a minimum age to qualify for a reverse mortgage. Federal law requires that a person be sixty-two or older."

"Ha!" Mitzy jumped to her feet again. "Samir was fifty-three! Five years ago, forty-eight. This reverse mortgage is not legal. So, you cannot own the property. My lawyer is going to have a, what do you call it? A feel day."

de Winter coughed lightly, but couldn't contain a smile from seeping through, then asked, "Mr. Reddick isn't your attorney?"

"It does not matter who he is, *Jackson*." Mitzy's eyes glowed.

de Winter gave her the sneer of an oily magician with one last card up his sleeve. "You're right, I don't care who Mr. Reddick is. Because the sale to me was legitimate, as was the reverse mortgage. You see, *Mitzy*, it wasn't taken out in Samir's name. It was taken out in the name of a man of the requisite age. A Mr. Markuss Vitolins."

Chapter 15

"So where is the $350,000?" asked Mitzy—a regular at 'Tanfastic'—stretching her bronzed gams across the sofa in her apartment.

"That's question number one," Cam said. He averted his eyes from her thighs. Mitzy's skirt had ridden up five inches above her knees. She had dropped Shane at his place after leaving de Winter's office, and had invited Cam for takeout Chinese. Slumped in a low armchair, he picked through the plate of Szechuan chicken on his lap. "de Winter said that Samir and Markuss had gone in as partners on the property before they took out the reverse mortgage. That makes sense—they needed Markuss because of his age and Samir because this apartment was his residence."

"*Our* residence." Mitzy ground her teeth. "de Winter says he writes the check to some partnership corporation. What happens to it from there? Did Samir get it all or did Markuss get a—what do you say?—a cut?"

"We can certainly ask him."

"Let us talk with him first thing tomorrow, if you have the time."

"I have Emma in the morning, but I'm free later on," Cam said. "The other question is why Samir tied up the home like this. He'd been making steady mortgage payments for twenty years, right?"

Mitzy sat up and smoothed out her skirt. "Yes." She stabbed a pork dumpling with a fork. "No matter how hard I try, I cannot figure out the chopsticks."

"Five years ago, he and Markuss contrive to take out this reverse mortgage," Cam said. "Samir must have needed a few extra thousand dollars a month to stay afloat. And then nineteen months ago, they sell the place, which gives him—or he and Markuss—a huge lump sum. Why?"

"Why, indeed. He spent time in prison, you know."

"For pulling cons. You've told me before."

"Of course. I need a drink. Would you like some rum?"

"No thank you." While Mitzy traipsed into the kitchen, Cam's thoughts flickered to the Cape May police file and "M.V + P.V. (child)" in particular.

Mitzy returned a minute later, two tumblers in hand.

She set one on the table. "In case you change your mind, and if not, I have saved myself a return trip for a refill." She laughed hoarsely.

"Mitzy," Cam said, leaving the tumbler alone. "How long have you known Markuss?"

"About ten years," she said. "There was another embalmer in the village years ago. He retires and Markuss just starts showing up." She sipped her drink. "I am sure there was more to it than that, but no need for me to pay attention to the staff. Or the part-timers like Markuss. Why do you ask?"

Cam set his plate on the table. A chopstick tumbled off and pitched across the wood until it crashed into a carton of rice.

"No reason," Cam said.

***

"What do you know about landfills?" Becka asked Cam.

"I know enough not to buy a house downhill from one. I hear the runoff makes a pretty toxic soup."

Becka had assembled a team of volunteers to help her cull through a fill ten miles west of Rusted Bonnet. The squad included Cam, Missy, Malika, Cam's mother Darby, Tabby Vasquez, Tabby's husband, and their two teenaged boys.

The owner of Freshwater Refurbishing—who Cam, Becka, and Missy referred to as "J. Dub's cousin"—had provided Becka with the name on the garbage truck that hauled away his trash. A supervisor at the waste company told Becka that it dumped its load at the fill that the team of nine was now facing in knee-high black rubber boots and elbow-length yellow gloves. As deputy chief of police, Kacey had greased the wheels with the landfill owner to allow the team of scavengers to hunt for the buried booty.

The daytime shift supervisor of the fill, who introduced himself as Thad Dodson, explained the operations and layout of the daunting ocean of refuse that lay before them.

"What you're looking at is seventy-five acres of footprint. Follow me." He turned and led the team down a rutted gravel track that traversed over clumpy hills covered with sod. "We bring in about half a million pounds of garbage a day. Between twenty-five- and thirty trucks'-worth. So, it's a decent size fill for the area, but not nearly what you'd see serving a major city."

"Are we walking over trash right now?" Tabby's husband asked.

"We are," the supervisor said. "This is capped garbage."

The hills reminded Cam of potatoes lumped into a burlap sack.

The group crested a hill some hundred feet higher than the parking lot. Cam peered out. Toward the bottom of the opposite side of the hill and to their right, a sea of refuse filled a space the size of a large playground. Two massive utility vehicles crawled over it like rovers exploring the Martian terrain.

"That's the tipping face," Dodson explained. "Landfills are built in sections we call phases. First, we excavate a phase, digging as deep as we can 'till we're about five feet above groundwater. Then we lay layers of clay, plastic, and sand on top to form the base."

"What about drainage?" Tabby's husband asked. He wore saggy jeans and a faded sweatshirt bearing an image of a monster truck.

"Sandwiched between the base layers are perforated pipes for rainwater runoff," Dodson said. "The dirty stuff—leachate —flows into what we call a sump there on the edge of the phase then gets pumped into a truck and taken to a treatment facility."

"Sounds very sophisticated," Malika said.

"It is. Most people still think of landfills like unruly trash heaps. But modern fills are engineered to the hilt." He nodded toward the tipping face. "Every day, we work a different area of the phase, called a cell. The day's trucks dump the trash in the cell and it gets spread out by the bulldozer down there then crushed by the other vehicle, a compactor."

To Cam, the compactor looked to be about twice the size of the bulldozer and had wide tires with what looked like, from the distance, blunted spikes on them. "Why's it called the tipping face?" he asked.

"Because that's the face of the dump hill where trucks tip their loads," Dodson said. "The portable fencing around the edges of the cell are to keep litter from blowing out of the day's work area. Plastic bags are the worst. All of the day's trash is compacted down then covered with a few inches of dirt to keep animals out and the smell down. The next day another layer is added on top of the dirt in the same cell. Once each cell of a phase is full, the phase is permanently capped. That's a layer of soil, plastic, compost then sod to prevent erosion."

"What are the pipes sticking up from the grass for?" Malika asked.

"Gas from the trash that's decomposing under the cap," Dodson said.

"So, are we stomping on my father's chest?" Becka asked.

"I'd like to do that with my boots," Malika muttered.

"Chest of silver, I mean," Becka clarified. "Somewhere under this grassy knoll?"

"No, ma'am," Dodson said. "You're in luck. Provided the trunk you're looking for was dumped during the week you mentioned."

"All I have for accuracy is the recollection of a boat refurbisher who whittles, but it'll have to do," Becka said.

"Well, we keep meticulous records and the tipping face that week was a cell right at the beginning of the current phase. We're pretty close to the end of it now. Had we already capped it, I wouldn't have been so keen to let you all poke around. Even now, it won't be easy. That compactor does a pretty mean job so everything's going to be dense. And, of course, there's the decomposition factor."

Dodson walked the group down the gravel track and then across a grassy stretch to an area about a hundred yards from the tipping face. The hum of the bulldozer and compactor were audible. "I stuck yellow flags around the cell this morning so its perimeter is marked. We go seven layers deep on each cell— one layer for each day of a week. Monday's at the bottom, Sunday on top."

"The boat refurbisher said his trash is picked up on Fridays," Missy said.

"Well, that's four levels better than Monday," Dodson said. "The cell next door is surrounded by red flags—please keep the trash you move from the yellow cell inside the red one. I'll have the 'dozer push it all back and even it out when you're done. Now, I have to get to my work, but remember we're doing you a favor so don't go and sue us if one of you gets hurt."

***

Despite a temperature in the low 20s, Cam was awash in perspiration thirty minutes after starting the dig. The stench of rotten and decayed food permeated his facemask.

The refuse was so compact, Cam felt like a 49er mining for gold. The team brandished pickaxes and shovels to break up and scoop away the top two layers of the cell's refuse and soil, then carted it to the adjacent cell in wheelbarrows. Working in orderly rows across the face of the cell, it took them hours to penetrate two days' worth of trash.

"Won't be long now," Cam said to no one in particular and chugged the last of his bottled water.

"Good thing we're looking for silver," Tabby said. "Pretty much anything else would've been completely flattened by that compactor."

"Hopefully the chest will be smashed open," Missy added.

Thirty minutes later, Becka shouted, "I think I see it!"

The group crowded around her. Cam peered down at the corner of a metallic green and gold steamer trunk etched with fish-scale scalloping jutting out from the surrounding detritus. Tabby's husband and Cam quickly set to the task of unearthing the trunk with their pickaxes and shovels. In less than fifteen minutes, Tabby's sons jumped into the moat they created and hoisted it up.

What had undoubtedly once been a beautiful trunk now

resembled a grotesquely twisted—albeit somewhat boxy—largemouth bass. Jagged metal gashes ripped through its lid.

Malika handed Tabby's husband the cordless metal cutter he'd brought. The big man donned a pair of protective glasses and powered on the handheld device. A six-inch circular blade revved into action and Vasquez guided the tool like a butcher expertly filleting a fish. In a matter of minutes, the trunk's wounds split open wide enough for him to grasp two edges of the tear with gloved hands and wrench the metal apart, creating a generous gap.

Nine pairs of eyes stared into the belly of the beast. Vasquez stepped back as Becka sat on her haunches and reached inside. She yanked out a ragtag assortment of makeshift padding—stained T-shirts, worn hand towels, and a tattered Christmas stocking with embroidered dog bones—and tossed the mess over her shoulder. Then she looked up at her mother, an avaricious gleam transforming her eyes to a jackal's.

Missy dropped to her knees beside the trunk and dipped her hands inside. She strained. "I can't even lift one," she said.

Tabby's husband saddled up to the trunk and hefted out an enormous slate-colored bar—over a foot long and several inches wide.

"Are there three?" Cam asked.

"There are," Missy said.

Sunday, February 14

Cam spent Valentine's Day morning hacking red velvet waffles into jagged hearts for Emma, then sledding at a nearby park.

At eleven o'clock, Kacey arrived on his doorstep. Despite Sundays being Cam's day with Emma, the "Snowflake Ball"—an afternoon dance for local Girl Scout troops—took precedence. He knew Emma would be one of the only girls not escorted by a father, but Kacey insisted on going. Cam hadn't protested.

"You look terrific," he said. Kacey had perched herself on a stool at the kitchen counter. She was dressed in a tasteful, knee-length, raisin-colored dress, an infinity scarf, and low heels.

"Thanks," Kacey said looking past him in the direction of the bathroom—they could hear Emma splashing in the tub.

Cam filled her in on the meeting he and Mitzy had with de Winter.

"Fascinating," she said. "Samir and Markuss as business partners and both men get stabbed."

"Maybe they were having a business meeting when the robber broke in," Cam said.

"Samir was stabbed three hours before Markuss."

"So maybe they were supposed to meet at eleven and that's the real reason Markuss went back to the funeral home. Only when he arrived, Samir was dead and the robber was still in the building."

"For three hours?"

Cam tapped a foot against the ground. "I've been thinking there was at least one insider involved, because of the lock on the mortuary cooler. But what if there was only one burglar—an outsider. He kills Samir then spends the next three hours trying every combination under the sun. Markuss returns to Paul Bearer's to talk secret partnership shop with Samir. The robber hears him and knifes him as well."

"Secret partnership?"

"It was a secret from Mitzy."

"True," Kacey said.

Cam filled a glass with water from the sink. "Would you like some?" he asked. "Or a Coke Zero?"

"I'm fine," Kacey said. "I executed the warrant on Blair

Lamb's house."

"Did you find green pills?"

"We did." She focused her eyes on his. "Officer Hodges and I, that is. Two full blister packs in a bathroom and a half-empty one in her purse. Along with the two you found at Paul Bearer's, that's five. Drug companies can't manufacture the stuff in the States, which is why she bought them from overseas."

"She admitted they were hers?" Cam pulled a sweater off over his head, still overheated from sledding, and tugged down his long-sleeved undershirt.

"Yes. That doesn't bode well for her—it's illegal to even possess Rohypnol pills in Michigan. I arrested her."

Cam raised his eyebrows. "Did she slip one into my drink?"

"That was the first question I asked her at the station. I went after her for a solid hour, but without much luck."

"She's a tough cookie to crack?"

Kacey smiled. "That's for sure. Eventually, she asked for an attorney, so I had to stop. But not before she told me that she was the only one who ever took the pills. According to her, she has trouble sleeping."

"Xanax or Valium aren't powerful enough?"

"Apparently not, if she's telling the truth. Rohypnol is ten times stronger than either of those."

"You don't believe her, do you?"

Kacey shook her head. "It's too coincidental that you got knocked out after having drinks with her." She steered her eyes toward a wall.

Is she jealous? Cam wondered. "Not to mention," he said, "if she used them to sleep, why were there packets hidden in a box of molded candy at the funeral home?"

"I asked. That's what prompted her to ask for a lawyer."

"So, what happens now?"

"I'll turn over what I have, including your statement, to the District Attorney's office. They can prosecute her for possession, which carries up to two years. But I doubt she'll get that much time unless I can prove she used it on somebody."

"My statement isn't enough?"

"For now, it's 'he said, she said.' Plus, you didn't actually see her drop a pill in your drink."

"What other explanation can there be for me passing out?" Cam bawled.

"Any attorney worth his salt could think of several, I'm sure. Besides, the prosecutor has a bigger problem if there are any red-blooded Y chromosomes on the jury."

"She's too attractive?"

"Ding, ding, ding." Kacey smiled. "I'm no lawyer, but I can sum up the defense's case in a single sentence: Why would someone as good looking as Blair need to stack the deck with any man?"

"Unless she was robbing them," Cam said.

"Mr. Reddick, can you please tell the jury what you found missing from your home the morning after you were allegedly drugged."

"Ugh. Not a thing." He began to slice a Granny Smith.

"And nothing in her townhouse screamed 'stolen' to me. So, chances are we're stuck with a possession charge. My guess is her lawyer will plead it down and she'll wind up with probation and a fine. Maybe a couple hundred hours of community service if we're lucky." Kacey sighed.

"Do you think she might keep stolen goods at Piper's? Them being neighbors and all."

Kacey cleared her throat. "I hadn't thought of that. But when I spoke to Piper about Samir's death I was in her home. She didn't hesitate to let me in."

"But she knew you were coming, right?"

"She did. I suppose she would've had plenty of time to hide stolen goods. And it's not like I saw any part of her house other than the foyer and family room. But other than proximity of their townhouses and a shared employer, I don't have anything that connects them."

In the distance, the sound of running water stopped.

"Do you need any help, honey?" Kacey shouted.

"No! I'm almost seven, you know!"

Kacey smiled at Cam. "She's already acting like a teenager."

And I missed almost six whole years, Cam thought wistfully, then checked himself. *When am I going to stop beating myself up*? He focused on slicing the apple.

"Speaking of thievery, we found Mrs. Bitter's ruby necklace," Kacey said.

Cam's palm slipped against the apple's skin. The paring knife in his other hand grazed his thumb. He jammed it into his mouth.

"I thought you'd be surprised," Kacey said. "Do you need a bandage?"

Cam slowly retracted the thumb from between his lips. No taste of blood. He examined the digit. "I'm fine. Where did you find it?"

"An appraiser called the police station in Oxford."

"A jewelry appraiser?"

"Yes, a very respectable one, according to the chief there." Oxford lay fifteen miles of dusty gravel roads to the west of Rusted Bonnet. "A Mrs. Edith Smithwick discovered the necklace in her recycling bin yesterday morning. Bernie interviewed her. A county truck had picked up the day before, but Edith didn't get around to fetching her bin until a day later. She told Bernie she figured the necklace was costume jewelry, given the size of the stone—'as big as a baby's fist.'"

"But she took it to an appraiser anyway."

Kacey nodded.

Cam bit into a slice of apple and extended his plate toward Kacey.

"No thank you. It's worth about $30,000."

He chewed slowly, swallowed, then said, "Someone robs a funeral home, killing one man and almost another in the process, then throws away a $30,000 necklace? That doesn't make sense."

"There is *one* explanation." Kacey scratched her chin with a nail. "I asked Mitzy this morning who arranged Mrs. Bitter's funeral. She said two of the woman's sisters and an adult son, Nigel...."

"Mommy, I'm ready!" Emma strutted into the kitchen. A white cotton dress with a stripe of embroidered miniature roses fell straight down her frame. The hem swept along the floor. "I need help with my shoes," she said. "The straps."

Cam's heart quivered. "You look beautiful, Emma," he said.

"Definitely," Kacey agreed. "Let's fix your hair first." She straightened Emma's locks under a sequined band then tackled her shoes.

"I want to take a picture of you two," Cam said and waved them toward the dining room.

"Can Bait be in it?" Emma squealed.

"Of course!" Cam lined up his ex-wife and daughter to the left of the goldfish's tank and snapped off a half dozen shots on his smart phone. "Perfect."

"Sweetie, go pack up your bag," Kacey said. "I'm bringing you home after the dance."

Emma twirled out of the room and disappeared into the bedroom she used at Cam's townhouse.

"She looks just like you," Cam said, walking back into the kitchen.

Kacey followed. "Except her eyes, those are all yours."

Cam blinked away the tears that had begun to well. After a moment, he said, "You were telling me about Mrs. Bitter's family."

"Right." Kacey rested a hip against the rail separating the kitchen from the dining room. "Mrs. Bitter's sisters told Mitzy that the ruby necklace was the woman's homage to her late husband. She'd worn it every day since he died. For eleven years."

"I can certainly see why they wanted to bury her with it."

"That's precisely what the sisters insisted on." Kacey's eyes sparked. "But what if $30,000 was worth more to the son than his mother's devotion to his father?"

The scenario raced through Cam's head. "If Nigel's the beneficiary to Mrs. Bitter's will, he might not want her buried with the necklace, because he can't sell it if it's six feet under." He paused, then added. "Of course, with jewelry like that, I'd be surprised if Mrs. Bitter didn't have other assets to bequeath."

"Greed knows no bounds," Kacey said.

"So, Nigel steals the necklace from his own mother's neck?"

"That's what I was thinking. Then he waits a few days and plants it for an elderly woman to find—someone more likely to 'do the right thing' and call the authorities than cash in on a windfall. The police deliver it to the rightful owner—Nigel Bitter, the heir."

"But only after his mother is safely in the ground."

"Exactly."

Cam strode past Kacey to Bait's tank. He flipped open the lid and shook a palmful of flakes into the water. "If he had the necklace in his possession, why ditch it? Why not just keep it?"

"Because he knew the police were looking for it. If he tried to sell it, he'd be linked to a murder."

"Still, Nigel took a risk leaving the necklace in this Edith woman's bin. Why not stick it where no one was likely to find it, then make an anonymous call to the police?"

"A tip is more suspicious."

"It's suspicious anyway," Cam countered. "And not to beat a broken record, but how would Nigel know the combination to the cooler where his mother's body was being stored?"

"That's the problem I'm having. We're back to an inside job, even if Nigel played a role."

"Are you going to bring him in for questioning?"

"The chief said I need more than a hunch, which means more digging. Tomorrow morning, I'm going to see if anyone who lives near Mrs. Smithwick has a security camera."

***

Markuss sat ramrod straight in a wooden chair. To one side, Jana—her curls seemingly riveted to her scalp—mimicked his posture, like the last two contestants in a spelling bee.

"I don't like the fact that *this* man is in my home," Jana said to Mitzy. It was just past noon and Mitzy had driven Cam to the Vitolins's Tudor east of Rusted Bonnet. They sat on the edge of a slouching paisley sofa in a room that featured an antique harpsicord.

"Come now, Jana," Mitzy said. "Cam had nothing to do with Markuss's attack. He's *helping* me." She appeared stone sober.

"That's what murderers do in the movies," Jana said. "Stay close so they can feed you misinformation!"

"Phooey," Mitzy said. "I've known Cam for some time, and his mother forever."

"Well, I'm not offering you cake," Jana said and clasped her hands in her lap.

Markuss rolled his eyes. "What can we help you with, Mitzy?"

"Did you see the news the other day?" Mitzy asked.

"Jackson de Winter tried to bulldoze my funeral home. I have never seen so many television cameras."

"Yes, we caught the six o'clock report," Markuss said without emotion. A paper plate holding a sliver of milky yellow cake rested precariously on one arm of his chair.

"You know perfectly well who Jackson de Winter is, yes?"

"I do," Markuss said.

"You and Samir sold him my home right out from under my nose!" Mitzy's face reddened.

Cam smiled—he'd have to remember that particular mixed idiom.

"Our corporate partnership sold the Paul Bearer property, yes." Markuss said, looking down his long nose at Mitzy. "What information *your* husband did or did not relay to you is none of *my* business."

Mitzy emitted a soft snarl. Cam put a hand on her shoulder. "Markuss, did you and Samir form the partnership so he could take out a reverse mortgage on the property?" he asked.

Markuss lifted the plate of cake from his chair and leaned forward. "You sound like you're trying to trick me into saying something. Did Samir and I form a partnership? Yes. Did the partnership take out a reverse mortgage? Yes."

"That was my inheritance," Mitzy blurted out. "You were bleeding it dry."

"Your inheritance?" Jana said softly, the crow's feet at the edges of her eyes deepening. "That sounds like a motive for murder if I ever heard one."

Markuss sat back and placed a hand on his wife's knee. "Now, Jana, stop."

"Did Samir pay you off for you to partner with him?" Mitzy asked through gritted teeth.

Markuss closed his eyes, took a deep breath, then opened them. "I suppose I can tell you. I assume his share passes to you, so any lawyer could work out the partnership details easily enough."

Mitzy glared at him.

"A little over five years ago, Samir asked me to become a silent partner in Paul Bearer's. The terms were simple. I didn't have to put any cash down, but agreed to tack my name onto some papers. Perhaps it was because I have perfect credit or, unlike him, I don't have a criminal record. Or maybe it was simply that someone my age could qualify for a reverse mortgage. I didn't ask. Under the terms of our deal, he kept the profits from funeral trade and continued to make payments on the primary mortgage. I was entitled to ten percent of the reverse mortgage payment—a little under $300 a month and ten percent of Samir's equity stake."

Cam calculated in his head. "So, Samir was getting almost three thousand a month from Comerica on the reverse mortgage before you sold out to de Winter."

"Correct," Markuss said. "And after the deal with de Winter closed, I received a check for my ten percent—$35,000. Samir took the rest."

"So, there *is* money left for me," Mitzy whispered.

"Samir collected $315,000. Whether there's any left now, I have no idea."

"Three hundred a month and a thirty-five thousand dollar bonus is a pretty hefty chunk of change for signing your name on some papers," Cam observed out loud.

Markuss shrugged.

Cam looked up at the wood-beamed ceiling, then asked, "Why did Samir need the money?"

"I have no idea," the older man replied. His eyes were flat.

"I do not believe that for a minute," Mitzy said. Her fingers coiled.

"I won't be embalming for Paul Bearer's any longer, seeing

as how it's going to become a strip mall," Markuss said. "So, I can tell you without hesitation that I don't give a rat's backside whether you believe me or not."

Chapter 16

"They were the exact same Roulands," Cam insisted. Intent on ridding his desk of long-ignored paperwork, Samantha had surprised him when she knocked on the door to the breadbox. "I came by to borrow a Shop-Vac to clean out Herb's car and I heard you rustling papers," she'd explained. Itching to tell Samantha in person about his trip to Windsor, Cam had jumped at the opportunity.

"You sure went through a lot of trouble," she said after he finished. "And expense. That fancy event couldn't have been cheap. And you spent the night in a hotel!"

"Yes, but I'm telling you," Cam urged, "I saw the paintings. Sunflowers, a river, and the crushed cars. Are you sure what you saw weren't prints?"

"Definitely not, at least as far as I could tell." Samantha was standing in the open doorway, chipmunk teeth pressed into her lower lip. "And this Ronald gentleman told you that Mrs. Galax used to house sit for the Sicklesons?"

"He did. And I confirmed it."

"Now how on earth did you manage that? I thought you were

pretending to be from a casino."

"There was a daughter. A grad student named Ashlie."

"I need a glass of sweet tea," Samantha declared. "Would you mind telling me in the 'pen?"

"No problem."

Cam scrubbed down the kitchenette's refrigerator while Samantha fixed her tea. "Ashlie had gone for a run while I was speaking with her parents," he said. "After I left, I saw her sitting on the side of the road, about three miles from their house. I thought she might be injured so I stopped."

"That's quite chivalrous," Samantha said, then muttered something that sounded like "about time," to Cam's ears.

"It turns out, she was just stretching," he said, ignoring the barb. "Apparently some people do that halfway through a run."

"Stands to reason. Sometime I stretch in the middle of a job." Samantha launched into a set of deep knee bends. "Loosens up the joints. You should do these."

Cam ignored the suggestion. "Ashlie and I talked for a good ten minutes. I steered the conversation to the Windsor art scene and hinted that the Galaxes were my neighbors here in Michigan. Ashlie said they used to run in the same social circle as her parents. So, I told her what Ronald told me, only I made it sound like Kamila Galax said it—namely, that she house-sat for Ashlie's parents."

"Clever. And she took the bait?" Samantha swirled sugar and tap water in a chipped Kalamazoo Hornet's mug then dipped in a tea bag.

"Isn't the water supposed to be hot first and then chilled after you steep the tea?" Cam ventured.

"I have no time for all of that. Now how about you answer my question. Did this girl take the bait?"

Cam smiled. "She did. Mimi Sickleson couldn't bear to let her houseplants go unwatered when they skied in Banff or ventured south for the Derby. And Kamila was her most trusted plant sitter."

"Oh my," Samantha said.

"Oh my is right. Two sets of identical paintings—one in Michigan, one in Windsor. One set must be forged, right?"

***

At nine-thirty, just as Cam was settling down with a bottle of Devil's Backbone in front of a classic *Thin Man* film, his smart phone buzzed.

"Cam, I need a huge favor." Kacey's voice sounded distressed.

"Anything," he said.

"Emma's already asleep. Can you come over and hunker down on the couch? I need to get to the hospital. There was another attempt on Markuss's life!"

Monday, February 15

Wool socks were no match for a window frame saddled with a hairline fracture. Cam's toes, dangling over the edge of Kacey's corduroy loveseat, tingled with cold. In the midst of uncomfortable slumber, he sensed movement and cracked open one eye. Cam spied Kacey quietly shedding her down jacket in the front hall. She started to creep up the stairs.

"Kacey," Cam whispered loudly. She turned and padded into the parlor where Cam was lying.

"I'm sorry I woke you," she said in a hushed tone.

Cam sat up, pushing his feet under the blanket. "You didn't, I was awake. Mostly anyway. Is Markuss all right?"

"He's pretty shaken, but yes. Do you mind if I change into my pajamas? I'll come right back down."

"Do you want me to make coffee?" He glanced at the wall clock. Two thirty-seven.

"Definitely not," Kacey said. She mussed his hair, turned, and darted up the stairs.

Cam rubbed sleep from his eyes, retrieved a glass of water from the kitchen, and returned to the loveseat. He tucked still-chilly feet under his backside and wrapped the blanket over his knees.

Three minutes later, Kacey—clad in a teal tank and long pajamas bottoms—bounced down the stairs and flopped into a brown leather armchair. She smelled of lavender soap.

"You're going to be cold," Cam observed.

"I'm used to it," Kacey said. "One of these days I'll get around to fixing that window."

"So, what happened?"

"Markuss was attacked in his home," Kacey said. "Jana ran out to pick up Thai for a late dinner while he took a shower. He'd been painting their bedroom."

"At his age?"

"He's not feeble, Cam. Besides, when I was walking through the crime scene, I saw one of those telescopic poles for the roller so it's not like he was up on a ladder. The whole house stunk of paint. Why anyone would do that in the middle of winter is beyond me."

"The windows weren't open?"

"They were cracked."

"Please tell me this wasn't a *Psycho*-style attack." A Hitchcock aficionado, Cam had seen every one of the man's films at least three times.

"Thankfully, he didn't get knifed again. Markuss said he'd just stepped out of the shower and was drying his face with a towel when everything went dark. Someone threw a pillowcase over his head and tried to choke off his air supply."

"He fought off the attacker?"

Kacey smiled. "According to Markuss, he played dead. After struggling for a few seconds, he said he realized he'd never be able to overpower the assailant. So, he pretended to lose his breath and collapsed to the floor."

"The guy didn't check his pulse?"

"I guess not," Kacey said. She pulled her knees to her chest and clasped her hands around them. "Markuss said he felt lightheaded and was too scared to get up from the floor. He lay prone on the tile with his eyes closed until he heard Jana."

"Did he go to the hospital?"

"Yes, he's still there. Jana called 9-1-1. The emergency room doc I spoke with said Markuss's throat presented as textbook suffocation. Plus, he had telltale marks on his neck."

Cam shuttered. "That sounds horrific. I don't suppose you found any fingerprints."

"The crime scene guys are looking. But whoever threw the pillowcase over Markuss's head took it with him."

"Do you have any idea how long he'll be laid up?" Cam stood and folded the blanket. He laid it on the arm of the loveseat and sat back down, on the end closest to Kacey.

"I don't know what kind of recovery time he's looking at, but the hospital's keeping him for twenty-four hours as a precaution. Jana's staying on a cot in his room, which is good, because we need to keep them out of their house to see if we can find anything."

"Do you have any idea who did this?"

Kacey sighed loudly. "I don't. We've been focusing on the theory that Samir's murder was part of a two- person plan—an outsider and an insider. And we hadn't ruled out the insider being Markuss or Samir himself."

"The outsider turns against his partner."

"Right."

"So, you think the person who tried to suffocate Markuss is the same person who attacked him last week?"

"That's what my gut's telling me. And now I'm leaning toward Markuss as the original inside man. Why else would the outsider go after him a second time?"

Cam arched his back. "True. Plus, Markuss going to the movies with Shane just smells like some sort of fabricated alibi. Let me play this out. Markuss not only knows the combination to the mortuary cooler, but when a body with expensive jewelry will be inside. Namely, Mrs. Bitter. There's an outside man, maybe someone who can fence the ruby necklace. Markuss and the outsider steal the necklace, but Samir catches them in the act. So, one of them stabs him. Then the outside man decides he doesn't want to split the proceeds, so he goes after Markuss."

"Correct."

"Why attack Markuss the first time? If the outside man is a fence, why not just sell the necklace and run off with the whole kitty?"

"I thought about that," Kacey said. "My best guess is that the outsider is local. Even if the necklace is worth thirty grand, that's not enough to retire on in the Caribbean. So, the only way to keep it all for himself is to do away with Markuss."

"And Markuss, despite knowing who assaulted him the first time, didn't turn the guy in because if he had, he'd be implicated in the robbery."

"And the murder."

"Right. So why did the outsider dump the ruby in a recycling bin?"

Kacey cringed. "I don't know. And I don't know why he'd try to kill Markuss a second time if neither had the necklace to fence."

Cam stood. "There are way too many holes. Plus, I can't help but think there's a connection to Jackson de Winter." He brought Kacey up to speed on the partnership.

"Cam, stop investigating!" Kacey scolded. "You can't just talk to anyone you want to about a man who's been murdered."

Cam held up his hands. "I just tagged along with Mitzy. She's leading this crusade, not me."

Kacey's face softened. "I still don't think the chief will like it."

"But it's good information," Cam protested.

"Yes, but we're gathering it, too. The chief was looking into de Winter's financial affairs. He would've found out in his own time."

"I guess the best I can say is that if he's upset, he should direct his anger towards Mitzy, not me."

"Somehow, I know that won't be the case."

Cam grunted.

"In any event, it is fascinating," Kacey said. "But why would de Winter want to do away with Markuss? If he paid for the land and building, he has the right to put up a strip mall as long as he gets the right permits."

"I doubt de Winter tried to suffocate Markuss. But the second attack happened right after Mitzy and I found out Markuss profited from Samir's financial dealings. We were the only people who knew about his slice."

"You said Shane went with you to de Winter's office."

"He did, but we left him up front with the secretary and she seemed clueless."

"Any chance that was an act and she tipped off Shane?"

"I doubt it. And Mitzy and I kept our mouths shut in front of him on the ride back to Rusted Bonnet."

"So your money's on Mitzy?"

Cam paced around the room. "Maybe. I don't know. Could she have done it herself, or with Shane?" *Or Chet*, he thought. "Let's say Mitzy wanted to speed along her inheritance. She pretends to be drinking heavily, then stabs Samir after I've gone for the night. Only she doesn't realize that Markuss came back until it's too late—he saw her do the deed."

"Markuss was stabbed close to three hours after Samir," Kacey said.

"Okay, so at eleven, Markuss sees Samir's dead body and goes upstairs to tell Mitzy. She goes wild—maybe she'd been drinking for real by then—so she grabs a second knife, chases him down, and tries to stab him, too. Then she steals the ruby necklace to throw off the police—a robbery gone sour. She doesn't want to get caught with the necklace or risk trying to sell it, so she dumps it in an elderly woman's recycling bin."

"So why didn't Markuss tell us that Mitzy was the one who assaulted him?"

Cam held a finger to his lips. "Maybe he didn't actually see her. Mitzy just thought he did."

"So, she didn't chase him down?"

"I don't know. Maybe she heard him come into Paul Bearer's and saw him standing over Samir's body. She sneaks up and attacks him."

"Then drags his body into the hall?"

"Why not?"

"So why try to suffocate him now?"

Cam took a moment to consider the question. "Because she learned he was in cahoots with Samir and she's already killed once. If she gets caught, she's getting life in prison anyway, so why not get rid of the other man who stiffed her out of her just deserts."

"Markuss isn't a spring chicken by any stretch. But he told me the person who threw the pillowcase over his head was strong."

"She had the element of surprise. Or Shane could have done it."

"Perhaps," Kacey said. "Plus, he's taller so it probably would've been easier for him. I'm going to call Samir's lawyer tomorrow. I want to know if he had the $315,000 nestled away in an account somewhere. I bet Mitzy's already made that call."

"Kacey, there's one other thing I have to tell you," Cam said. He rubbed a toe against the kilim rug. "If Mitzy is the attacker, it's possible that Chet Szubek is the man she's working with." He explained what he'd heard and seen three nights earlier.

"What were you doing in Paul Bearer's that late at night?" She slammed a hand against the arm of her chair. The smack of skin against leather jolted Cam.

"Following my mother's advice," he said sheepishly. "To look there for the ruby."

"Darby told you to break into someone's home in the middle of the night?"

"It wasn't the middle of the night."

"It was night time and more to the point, you broke in."

"The door was unlocked and I'm there all of the time."

"I can't believe you."

"Yes you can." Cam tried his best smile.

Kacey raised her eyes to the ceiling then rolled her neck and said. "If the chief finds out, I'll have to arrest you."

Can sighed.

"Chet and Mitzy?" Kacey asked after a long pause. "He must be at least twenty years younger than her."

"It is what it is."

"She brainwashed him into killing her husband for her?"

"Why not? And he was a star hockey player, so he's definitely strong enough. Can you find out if he's in Chicago tonight? That's where he lives."

"I don't think so," Kacey said. "If he becomes a viable suspect, we can try to verify his whereabouts later, but I can't justify calling Chicago P.D. and having a cop bang on his door at three in the morning without anything more to go on."

"Too bad. If he's cleared, do you have to tell Bernie?"

Kacey grumbled, "I guess not," then said, "It's late. Do you want to spend the rest of the night here?"

Cam peeked at the clock. "No, I'll take off. That'll make it easier for you to do the morning routine with Emma. Unless you want to sleep in—I could handle getting her off to school."

"No, thanks, I'll be fine."

Cam stood and stepped softly to the front closet to retrieve his coat.

Kacey followed him. "There's one other angle that keeps nagging at me," she said as he twisted the handle.

"What's that?"

"I don't know why I keep telling you things. It only gives you more to go on."

"Come on," Cam said. "I'm only trying to help."

"I know, but one of these days it's going to get me into real trouble," Kacey said. "It's just that I can't stop thinking about Samir. *He's* the former con man. *Not* Markuss or Mitzy or Chet, or even Shane."

"True."

"A valuable necklace is stolen and later dumped, and Samir had a lot of cash—or at least he did nineteen months ago. Things don't add up. I keep going back to the 'keep it simple, stupid' rule we learned in the academy—if something seems obvious, it's probably correct. In this case, that Samir tried to pull a new con and it got him killed."

Chapter 17

"I can't sleep, Bait," Cam said at five in the morning.

The goldfish whipped through a synthetic pineapple.

"I guess you can't, either." Cam sipped freshly ground coffee in front of the fish's tank. "Or maybe I woke you with the light. Sorry."

He warmed his hands around his mug. Cam hadn't turned his heat up past 68 degrees and the chill cut through his T-shirt. "I think Kacey's right. I have to focus on Samir. And that means the money and the ruby."

Bait zipped from one side to the other then settled toward the bottom of the octagonal tank.

"I think you're right. Maybe I should pay Nigel Bitter a visit this afternoon and see what he has to say about the ruby."

***

"It must be nice to have a long weekend at home," Cam said. Runny eggs and hot sauce on his indigo blue plate evoked images of Edvard Munch, or more aptly, screamed his name. He and Samantha were seated on one side of a booth in a downtown Windsor café.

"It's comfortable," Ashlie Sickleson replied. "Whenever I come home, I'm reminded of how good my life is—parents who love me, zero pressure from them, and as much financial support as I need. Not that I intend to be dependent on them forever." She sliced a wedge of cantaloupe with surgical precision.

Cam could feel Samantha shift in her seat next to him. She maintained her focus on a cinnamon roll the size of a small pumpkin, oozing with glaze. On countless occasions, Cam had heard her opine on the offspring of Peachy Kleen's wealthiest clientele.

"Are you following your parents' footsteps into the art world?" Cam asked. He had located and messaged Ashlie on social media, insisting that he had a sensitive topic to discuss with her. She had responded promptly, but seemed skeptical when Cam asked her to meet him for breakfast. She must have figured it was a veiled request for a date, he thought—until he asked if he could bring along his fifty-five-year-old colleague.

"I don't have an eye for it, or the interest," Ashlie said. She sipped chocolate milk from a straw. "I'm in journalism school at Ryerson."

"In Toronto?"

"Yes." She brightened. "Most people from the States haven't heard of it." Ashlie shifted her focus to Samantha, who had just lodged a jawbreaker-sized hunk of bun into her cheek—like an overambitious squirrel.

Samantha raised a napkin to her lips.

"So, what's on your mind?" Ashlie asked, not directing the question to either Cam or Samantha in particular.

Sensing his co-worker's labor to chew, Cam recounted the

tale of Samantha's discovery in the Galaxes's attic. He finished with, "They're identical to the three Roulands in your parents' house."

"So, you were full of you-know-what when you told my parents you're working with the casino?" Ashlie asked Cam.

He nodded nearly imperceptibly, fearing that she would jump to her feet and storm off.

But Ashlie's eyes twinkled. A fleck of Dijon colored her brown sugar irises. "Are Gannon and Kamila Galax criminals?"

Cam shrugged, but Samantha rocketed her head up and down. "Yes!" she said between pursed lips.

Ashlie stabbed her fork into a slice of cantaloupe. "This could be the break I need—do you have any idea how hard it is to land a position as an investigative reporter?" A smile dripping with ambition stretched across her chapped lips. "If this pans out, goodbye research internship in Kingston, hello CBC Toronto."

Samantha finally swallowed. "Good, dear," she said. "Now, all we need is an art appraiser to pay a little visit to your parents' house."

***

"I can't talk now, I have to go arrest Shane and Jelly Roll," Kacey exclaimed. She was moving fast.

Cam pushed himself away from the knotty pine wall in the police station lobby. Bookended by photos of Bernie with a former mayor of Detroit and of a solitary, snow-garbed pine tree with an award ribbon tacked to the bottom of the plastic frame, he had been waiting to tell Kacey about Gannon and Kamila Galax.

Cam followed her out the front door. "Arrested? For what?"

"Sorry, I don't have time to explain." Kacey slid into her

cruiser, ratcheted the door shut, and sped off.

Cam kicked the pavement. Most of the snow had melted under a few days of merciful sun and temperatures in the mid-40s. After a moment's consideration, he strode back into the station.

"Hope," he whispered loudly to the desk clerk, "Kacey said she's arresting Shane Orucov and Jelly Roll Sands. Do you have any idea why?"

The bottled redhead looked up from a tattered King James Bible. "Now, Cam," she said in a hushed tone, "You know I can't talk to the *citizenry* about police work." Her desk sat behind an internal window to the lobby.

Cam stepped closer to the desk and offered Hope Winchester his best puppy dog eyes. "I'm just trying to help Kacey any way I can. She has so much on her plate between this job and Emma." Hope—a forty-something mother of two and wife of the village's Lutheran pastor—had been among the first in Rusted Bonnet to welcome Cam home a year earlier. Others in the small town had snubbed him—a heel who had abandoned his young wife and child. But on his first weekend after returning, at a community spaghetti dinner that Darby had encouraged Cam to attend, Hope had given him a motherly hug and encouraged him to live a good 'Christian' life. If you do, "the villagers will come around," she had promised, not that Cam was religious.

"How does your knowing help Kacey?" she asked, carefully placing a gold-leafed bookmark between pages in the Bible. Her fingernails were painted a garish electric blue.

Cam scanned the empty waiting room. "You know I helped on that other murder case a while back, right?" he asked softly.

Hope bobbed her head.

"I don't have to adhere to the same protocols as the police," Cam said.

Hope's eyes widened. "You're not doing anything illegal, are you?"

"No, no," Cam assured her. "It's more like I'm a private investigator. They don't have to jump through as many hoops when they ask questions." In a conspiratorial tone, he added, "It makes it easier to put pressure on suspects."

"That makes sense." Hope's eyelashes flickered. "So, you think Shane and Jelly Roll killed Mr. Orucov? And attacked Mr. Vitolins? Twice!"

"It's possible," Cam said. "Why's Kacey bringing them in?"

Hope swiveled in her desk chair to verify that the area behind her was vacant, then completed the circle. "The officer on the scene said he caught the two of them taking crow bars to a car," she said quietly. "They smashed in the windshield, dented the doors, and broke all of the mirrors. That's big-time destruction of property."

"Whose car was it?"

Hope flicked her eyes down at a note pad on her desk. "The officer ran the license plate. It belonged to someone named Jackson de Winter."

***

"I'm worried about Afya," Malika said. She still called Becka by the name she'd given her at birth.

Cam had joined Malika at a home on the western edge of Rusted Bonnet to help her move an armoire. An inquisitive kitten had upended an open bottle of rubbing alcohol that Malika was using to remove dried fingernail polish from the hardwood of a teen's bedroom floor. The alcohol cut a path straight under an antique maple armoire. While colorless, Malika didn't want to simply leave the liquid.

"You could've taped a cloth around a yardstick and slid it

under," Cam had said when he saw the vintage piece. Its legs raised the body less than an inch from the floor—not high enough to reach under with a hand, but Cam found yardsticks to be a useful cleaning resource.

"I did consider something like that," Malika had responded, "but I want to tip the armoire forward, too, to wipe the bottom of its hind legs in case any alcohol found its way there. It would be a shame to damage any part of this gorgeous furniture because I didn't remember there was a kitten prowling underfoot."

"You can't be blamed for that," Cam had said and helped her heft the armoire.

After ensuring that the floor and legs were dry, Malika sat on the edge of the teen's bed and raised her concern about her daughter. She wore a brightly-colored scarf wrapped around her head.

"Why are you worried?" Cam asked. He leaned against the armoire. "She seems to be doing incredibly well. Of course, I only see her professional side."

"It's these bars of silver. Since receiving the correspondence from her father, the silver is all she talks about. She glossed right over his confession."

"She had already figured all of that out," Cam noted. "When she found you."

"Yes, I know. But she wasn't moved in any direction by his written words—not sadness or anger or even pity. She fixated on the treasure."

"The bars are worth a lot of money," Cam said.

"Yes, but newfound money can make people act in ways they are not accustomed to acting. Ways that require even more money."

"What has Becka said?"

"That she wants to buy a better car and make a down

payment on a house and go to the Caribbean with Missy. She already bought a new tablet and television and tickets to some music festival all on credit and she hasn't even sold the bars yet. Forty-five thousand dollars is a lot of money, but it won't last forever."

"And you're worried that she'll wind up in debt?"

"Yes. Windfall turned to downfall. That's my worry."

***

Between a ski slope nose and equine teeth, Nigel Bitter hadn't been bestowed with any maker's benevolence in the looks department. Cam had located Nigel's address in the online White Pages and simply knocked on his door, not expecting him to be home on a Monday afternoon. But to his surprise, a man answered.

Wearing a leopard print bathrobe and fuzzy slippers, Nigel introduced himself and invited Cam inside not even knowing who he was. Ten minutes later, Cam was enjoying hot mulled cider—wassail as Nigel called it—in a kitchen close to the size of Emma's first grade classroom. After asking Cam about himself, Nigel—a self-proclaimed "speed trader" on every market from the Americas to Asia—had launched into an exegesis on the finer points of commodities, not that Cam had inquired. Apparently, sugarcane futures had gone haywire that morning.

"So how do I not know you?" Nigel finally asked.

"I grew up here," Cam said, "but I moved away for a while. Have you lived in Rusted Bonnet long?"

Nigel, who appeared a number of years older than Cam, said, "For about five years. I burned out in New York. Investment banking. So, I chucked the lifestyle and went in for this old farm house to be close to my mother after she moved into an assisted living facility." He sipped wassail from a ceramic mug. "Would you like a scone? I bake them myself."

Cam accepted and Nigel added a dollop of clotted cream on a small China plate alongside a pair of scones. He handed the offering to Cam.

"Thank you," Cam said and bit into a scone. The flavor of currants tickled his tongue. "This is phenomenal."

"Black currant is one of my favorites. I make a good savory one with Gruyere, too."

"It was a shame about your mother. I happened to be cleaning Paul Bearer's while she was there." He described Peachy Kleen.

"So, are you here soliciting business?"

"No. I actually wanted to ask you about your mother's necklace."

The top of Nigel's robe had loosened, presenting a mat of dark hair plastering his chest. "How did you know about that?" He blinked rapidly.

A nervous tic? "I think the whole village knows it was stolen on the night Samir Orucov was murdered," Cam said. "And that it turned up in a recycling bin. Plus, my ex-wife's a police officer."

Nigel's eyes drooped at the mention of an ex-wife. After a heartbeat, he asked, "What did you want to know?"

Cam weighed his options. He didn't dare ask Nigel if he had stripped the ruby from his dead mother's neck. Instead, he said, "I have a friend who works at an auction house in Chicago. I was wondering if you plan to sell it."

Nigel swirled a demitasse spoon in the glass jar of clotted cream. "The thought never crossed my mind."

Was he telling the truth? "I'd love to see it," Cam tried.

Nigel touched the tiny spoon to his tongue. "I thought you said you saw my mother while she was at the funeral home."

This man is no fool. "I did," Cam said. "I'm sorry, I really should be going."

Nigel held up a hand. His fingernails were surprisingly dirty. "No, stop. That was rude of me. Mother's necklace isn't here. She wanted to be buried with it, but, of course, that didn't happen. So once the police retrieved it, I did the next best thing. I gave it to my aunts to share."

***

Cam relayed his interaction with Nigel to Kacey over their second bowl of ice cream at her kitchen table. He'd brought Moose Tracks, real fudge, and a jar of Maraschino cherries—Kacey's favorite—"just because." Emma had been delighted to see Cam and, after devouring a sundae, spent the better part of an hour showing off her latest skill set—playing Chopsticks on her maternal grandmother's upright piano that now resided in Kacey's basement. Once Emma had settled into bed for the night, Cam and Kacey decided a second round of Moose Tracks was in order.

"You shouldn't have gone to Nigel's house," Kacey said. "I haven't spoken with him yet."

"I know, sorry. But as long as Nigel's aunts verify his story, you can drop him from your suspect list."

Kacey wiped a bead of fudge from the edge of her bowl and licked her finger. "Because robbing your mother's dead body doesn't jibe with giving up the loot to a pair of aunts?"

"Exactly."

Kacey hummed. "You said Nigel is intelligent, right?"

"Very much so."

"Suppose he steals the necklace but gets caught and stabs Samir in a fit of panic. Then intelligence and raw survival skills take over, trumping greed. He figures that bestowing the necklace on his aunts put him above suspicion."

"Yikes," Cam said.

"Leave the detecting to the pros, Cam. I was going to speak with Nigel this morning, but I got sidetracked by Shane and Jelly Roll. They destroyed Jackson de Winter's car."

Cam played dumb—he didn't want to cause trouble for Hope or more for himself. "Now, why would they do that?"

"I think they were just taking out their frustration. de Winter crushed Shane's fantasy of running the funeral home, not that Mitzy would've turned over the keys to the castle. And Jelly Roll couldn't get his job back with the Catholic place after telling them to pound sand."

"Is de Winter pressing charges?"

"Definitely. But the prosecutor is likely to go easy on them. Well, Shane at least. He gave up Blair."

"What?" Cam jerked his head upright.

Kacey's smile stretched wide. "Shane told me he had dirt on Blair and asked if he could use it for leniency."

"Maybe he's not so dumb after all."

"He credited Netflix for the idea. Blair's running a burglary scheme."

"But she didn't take anything," Cam protested.

"The plan's a little more sophisticated than that. You'll want to change your locks by the way."

Cam jabbed his spoon into his ice cream. "It sounds like Paul Bearer's was a con artists' colony."

Kacey laughed. "That's for sure." She bit into a cherry and laid the stem on a napkin beside three others. "Shane told me about a guy who lives up in Bay City. Devon Schuler, but he goes by 'Taco.'"

"Seriously, Taco?"

"Seriously. He's a burglar by trade. Shane introduced Blair and Taco a few years back." She dribbled juice from the

Maraschino cherry jar onto her ice cream. "Blair's been running a racket, using Taco to get paid. According to Shane, she hits the bars alone. With her looks, she knows she'll be approached by dozens of men. When one comes on to her who's expensively dressed, she plies him with drinks and a roofie. She goes to his place, making sure he doesn't black out until she's seen him punch in the alarm code, then drags the guy up to his bedroom, strips him down to his underwear, and leaves him to sink into oblivion. But she doesn't sleep with him or rob him of anything other than a house key. She runs to a 24-hour place that duplicates keys, has a set made, and returns the originals to the man's pants pockets. Later, she sells a neat little burglary package to Taco—address, house key, and alarm code. According to Shane, she gets twelve hundred for every mark. The rule between them is that Taco never goes in to rob the place until at least six months have passed. That way, the guy doesn't connect the incidents."

"And no one has ever gone to the police?"

"For the robberies, they all do."

"But not because they suspected that Blair slipped something in their drink?"

"Not that I'm aware of. I have to admit, Blair in the point position has flair—it plays right into a guy's ego. He wakes up the next morning in his skivvies, vaguely remembering having drinks with an incredibly attractive woman. He does the mental math and assumes he got lucky, only she took off before he woke up. He chastises himself for not remembering what must have been the best sex of his life, then pats himself on the back for the feat. His main regret is that he never got her number to repeat the night's event."

"And he'd have no reason to suspect anything was amiss, because Blair didn't steal a thing. His keys aren't even missing."

"Exactly." Kacey touched her tongue to her spoon. "But she messed up by using a bar in Rusted Bonnet and trying to pull the scam on someone she knew. Namely, you."

Cam smiled. "I'm typically not one to pass out after three drinks. But I can understand how it worked with other men. If I hadn't seen the roofies in her handbag, it never would've crossed my mind that she drugged me." He paused, then added, "I noticed her demeanor change when I told her I owned Peachy Kleen and how many clients we had."

Kacey looked down at her ice cream. "Did you think you slept with her?"

"Not really." Cam's face pinkened to the color of Hawaiian Punch. "What's going to happen to her?"

"Between your statement and Shane's, she should see some jail time. I contacted Bay City P.D. and they're picking up this Taco person. I'm not sure if the prosecutors will see Blair or him as the bigger fish to fry. They may go hard after both." She inspected a cuticle, and began to pick at it. "I'm worried that this case might get hyped up by the media."

Cam ran a hand through his flaxen hair. "Why's that?"

"Gorgeous woman, a horde of duped men, a devious partner. It has a lot of sex appeal. I wouldn't be surprised if some of the lower brow national news reporters come flocking."

"Oh, boy."

"Oh, boy is right. I definitely need to talk with the chief about how to handle it."

Chapter 18

Cam needed a drink like a street needs a pothole. But after leaving Kacey's, Mitzy texted, insisting that she needed his help moving a piece of furniture to the curb. It sounded to him like a pretext for drinks. He had no interest in becoming Chet's successor, but he couldn't pass up the chance to find out if she knew anything else about why Shane and Jelly Roll destroyed de Winter's car.

Cam rapped on the front door of Paul Bearer's, then glanced at his watch: ten after nine. He half expected Mitzy to answer in a nightie. But when she pulled back the door, her slinky figure was sheathed in a Red Wings jersey that fell to her knees and skinny jeans. With her dark hair tied back and a pinch of color in her cheeks, Mitzy might have looked closer to Cam's age than his mother's, except for her eyes—glazed discs that failed to focus even when directed straight at his. Cam followed her inside, where she promptly plucked a tumbler from a tall table in the vestibule.

"Let us go into the lounge," she said and led him into the octagonal room near the front of the funeral home. A bottle of

Knob Creek, bottles of ginger beer, and bitters festooned a glass-topped coffee table. Mitzy topped off her glass with the bourbon, then fixed Cam a drink and handed it to him. "Sit," she directed.

He perched at the edge of a half-moon shaped, dusty-blue sofa. Mitzy positioned herself at the other end and slung one leg over her opposite knee.

"Where's the armoire you needed help with?" Cam asked.

"Upstairs," Mitzy purred. "But it can wait."

Cam squirmed.

"Did you hear what my brilliant boy got himself into?" she asked and sipped bourbon.

"I did." Cam brought his tumbler to his nose. It twitched reflexively.

"You do not like the bourbon?" Mitzy asked.

"It's fine," Cam said. "I'm just not in a drinking mood tonight."

Mitzy smiled, her thin lips stretching wide. "Too bad. I am."

Cam took a shallow breath. "Do you know why Shane and Jelly Roll went after de Winter's car?"

"Because they are immature. They do not get what they want and they look for revenge. Samir is dead so Mr. Jackson the third is the next best thing for them, I think." She looked at her glass and took another sip. "I spoke with Samir's lawyer today. My S.O.B. husband did exactly what de Winter said. Reverse mortgage with Markuss then sold this *palace* to de Winter." She swept her hand holding the tumbler toward the door. Booze flew from her glass onto the carpet. "Ha!" Mitzy shook her head. "What do I care? I am leaving soon." She reached toward the bottle of Knob Creek, but fell six feet short. "Would you be a dear?"

"Why don't you finish mine first," he said, sliding across the sofa toward her. They exchanged glasses. Cam moved back to his side.

"You do not want to sit next to me, Cammie?"

"I don't think that's a good idea."

She stretched an arm across the back of the sofa. "Because I have been drinking or you are not attracted to an old lady?"

"It's not right for any number of reasons," Cam said. "One of which is that your husband just died."

"Ach! That no-goodnik. You know how much he left me? The lawyer gave me access to his hush-hush bank account. A fat twelve thousand left. That will not last long. The son-of-a-rat."

"Did the lawyer tell you what he spent it on?"

"He did not know. But those every-month bank payments and big daddy check from Mr. the third are gone. Poof!" She downed half of the drink in her hand. "Twelve grand for Mitzy and no place to live. I will maybe fly to Baku and move in with my sister. She is a—how do you say it?—spinster. Ha! I will be a spinster, too. Or maybe I can find a rich man. Not con man rich. Respectable rich." Her head lolled down. As soon as her chin struck the top of her chest, she jerked it back up. "And no little Pipers running around with my new man."

Cam shifted in his seat. "Piper and Samir?"

"Oh, I do not think so for real. Maybe he fiddles a little bit, that is all. I think she always wants more money. A raise, a raise, always asking for a raise. So, she follows him around and does what he says."

Basically, doing her job as well as yours, Cam thought. "Did Piper do whatever Markuss wanted as well?" he asked, wondering—as Kacey had—if she could be his daughter.

"Markuss?" Mitzy slammed back the rest of her drink, then said, "No, no. She calls him an old fool. No common sense she says. I think because he is always forgetting things. His keys, his winter gloves."

His wallet, Cam thought. "So, he was like a space cadet?"

"I do not know what that means?"

"That he was spacey? Not all together there all of the time."

"Oh, I wouldn't think that, just maybe he forgets things. I think he can do his job. But who knows—they are in the ground so if he does not embalm the right way, no one can know to complain!" She laughed. "I need a refill," Mitzy uncrossed her legs, pressed her knees together at a slight angle, and shook her empty glass in the air. *Queenly.*

"I'm not sure how much of the ginger beer or bitters to add," Cam said, standing and taking the tumbler from her hand.

"No need for those. Just pour in *the juice.*"

Taking advantage of Mitzy's obvious inebriation, Cam asked, "I noticed Chet Szubek hanging around here this past week."

"Did you now?" Mitzy's lips curled upward. "His mother and I used to go to the races," she said flippantly.

"Races?" Cam repeated and filled the tumbler with Knob Creek, then handed it to Mitzy.

"Harness racing in Hazel Park. Steffi knew her horses. Of course, she liked losers!" She chortled.

Cam assumed she was referring to Samir.

"She grew up with what is-it-called? The 4-H," Mitzy added. "Used to show horses at the Armada Fair. English, I think. Or maybe it was Western."

"But you grew apart?"

"How did you know that?"

"You told me," Cam said.

Mitzy took a drink of straight bourbon. "Just the way I like it." She smiled. "I suppose I did. Steffi changed her tune about me, that is for sure." She cackled.

"Why's that?" Cam asked and sat down.

Mitzy wagged a finger. "No, no, that is not for you to know."

"She slept with Samir."

Mitzy's face reddened, but she said nothing.

"So you slept with her son." Cam stated.

Mitzy sipped more liquor then blurted out, "I plead a fifth!" with a laugh.

Bang, bang, bang! A pounding noise sounded on the front door.

"Saved by the door!" Mitzy shouted. "Who could that be at this hour?"

"Chet?"

"No, that boy has run back to Chicago."

"Shane? Kacey told me he was granted bail."

Bang, bang, bang! Louder.

"Shane has a key. Would you mind?"

Cam stepped into the vestibule. *Bang, bang!* Solid wood rattled. The door had no peephole.

"Who's there?" Cam called out. He sensed a presence behind him and looked over his shoulder. Mitzy leaned against the doorframe between the vestibule and lounge. Her knees wobbled. They didn't look like they could support her weight much longer.

"A man you don't trifle with," a heavily-accented male voice said from the other side of the door.

"That sounds-s like Jalil," Mitzy slurred. "Samir's brother."

***

Jalil stood six inches taller than Cam's six-foot frame. His V-shaped chin and almond-shaped eyes sparked the image of 'cartoon alien' to Cam's mind. But a light beard and plum-colored skin tempered the similarity.

After proffering her brother-in-law an awkward hug, Mitzy had implored Cam to stay. Jalil lugged a tattered suitcase up the stairs to the apartment and upended it in the center of Mitzy's snow-white living room carpet. From his feet, he removed boots more befitting a *Mork & Mindy* sketch than modern day America.

"What are you doing here?" Mitzy demanded and tossed Jalil's boots to the rug in the foyer with a pair of underhand throws.

"I came to get Samir's remains, seeing as how you said in your e-mail that you didn't want them." He sat on the sofa.

His English is better than Mitzy's, Cam thought.

"I could have mailed you his damn ashes," Mitzy spat back. She rocketed into the kitchen and returned with a glass that looked like it was filled with water. "He is more stupid than Shane," she whispered in Cam's ear then wilted into an armchair. She closed her eyes.

"That one is always passed out," Jalil said to Cam. "She drinks all of the time but cannot hold her liquor." He poured himself a tumbler of bourbon from the bottle on the table in front of him.

"Unlike you, right?"

"This is nothing!" Jalil laughed. He downed the glass and refilled it. "I could finish the bottle, but I won't."

Cam glanced at Mitzy. She had started to lightly snore. "Perhaps I should go," he said.

"I'm not tired so I don't care one way or the other," Jalil said. "I slept on the airplane. All three legs."

"That seems like a long way to come. Have you been here before to visit?"

"Twice. Once when Samir was in...."

"I know about his past," Cam said.

Jalil shrugged. "Samir is smart. He only went to prison one time. Me, I've been inside three times in Baku." He narrowed his eyes at Cam. "Are you a *friend* of Mitzy's?"

"Not like that," Cam said quickly. "I own a housekeeping

business. Samir and Mitzy were clients. She asked me to help her move furniture. But really, I think she's just lonely."

"I'm not surprised. I don't think she's the type to have girlfriends. Am I right?"

"I don't know her that well, but I don't recall seeing her spending time with other women."

"Me, neither."

"Have you been in Rusted Bonnet before?"

"Yes, I've been here once. And to Kansas when my brother was in prison."

"Did they ever visit you?" Cam, who'd been leaning against the wall, sat in an armchair matching the one Mitzy occupied.

"One time. Maybe fifteen years ago. Mitzy's father died. Lung cancer. Two packs a day will do that to anyone. They haven't been back since. But Samir and I, we keep in good touch. *Kept* in good touch, I suppose I should say now." Jalil poured himself a third tumbler of bourbon.

After engaging in twenty minutes of banter and replenishing Jalil's glass twice more, Cam mustered his resolve. "Samir used to tell me about his days in Baku when you two were pulling cons to get yourselves off of the street," he said, stretching the truth—Samir had never been so direct with him.

"Those were the good times!" Jalil replied with relish. "We never got caught. Samir had a good head on his shoulders. He taught me enough to get by."

"All but three times?"

Jalil stared blankly at Cam.

"The three times you went to jail," Cam said.

"Oh, right." He took another drink, dribbling half of a mouthful down his chin. "This stuff is stronger than I thought."

"Did you ever look for regular work?"

"What, like selling insurance? No way. It's not in my DNA." He squinted at Cam. "Do you happen to know who Mitzy's lawyer is?"

Cam straightened up, sensing an opportunity to suss out a tidbit of information. He was stone sober. "I don't, though she told me she met with him today," he replied.

Jalil's eyes glowed a fiery yellow. "I need to speak to this-s man," he slurred.

"Are you in Samir's will?"

"I'm not sure about that. But Samir promised me just a little bit more."

"More?" Cam asked. "Has he been supporting you?"

Jalil looked away, then said, "Support isn't the right word." He rose, stabilizing himself with one hand on an arm of the sofa, then grimaced. "Arthritis. Even the booze doesn't stand in its way." He raised a hand in a good-bye gesture, said, "I'll get the lawyer's name from Mitzy tomorrow morning, whether she likes it or not," and wobbled off toward the guest bedroom.

Chapter 19

"These are photographs."

The words oozed from Emil Zieler's lips like glistening cheese pumped into a plastic tray of ballpark nachos, landing with a glop in Cam's ears.

Adorned in hipster glasses and a scarf the color of raspberry jam, the art appraiser touched his forefinger to the hood of a pink crushed car above the Sickleson's great room fireplace. "Feel this." He gently took Ashlie's wrist and guided her fingers toward the painting. "Now, come this way." Emil directed her to the left of the mantle as Cam and Samantha stood on, watching.

Ashlie brushed her index finger against the corner of a second painting, one of a Monarch resting on milkweed. "It feels different," she said.

"They *should* be the same type of paint—gouache. That's acrylic mixed with gum arabic, a binding agent. It's what makes the paintings opaque. Of course, top notch artists like

Rouland and Cheverson here," he said, pointing at the milkweed, "mix their own paints. But still, the textures should be similar. These aren't even close. In my professional opinion, all three of these Roulands are high-end digital photographs. Of course, there are chemical tests that can be run for verification." He glared at the crushed cars. "The replicas are quite good. I can see how they could fool a lay person, even one who has an appreciation for talent. Especially because gouache dries smooth, unlike oils. But let me assure you, these Roulands are not originals."

Samantha strode to the fireplace and pressed two fingers against the picture over the mantle then maneuvered around Emil and Ashlie and pushed a thumb squarely onto the Monarch's thorax. "Definitely different," she declared.

Cam didn't touch either work. But he studied each in turn for a long moment, his nose just inches from the pictures. "I can see it now that I know what I'm looking at," he finally said. "Ronald Tremblay told me that Gannon Galax had been a photography professor at the university."

"And Kamila house sat here for my parents," Ashlie said.

"Time to call the cops," Samantha announced.

"You and Oliver really nailed this one out of the park," Cam said.

Samantha beamed then turned to stare at a box of Godiva chocolates on a three-tiered, glass coffee table.

Ashlie followed her gaze. "Would you like a cup of coffee, Mrs. Krause? And perhaps a chocolate or two?"

"No thank you on the coffee, Miss. Sickleson. Gives me heartburn! Well, not the coffee we have at Peachy Kleen, but that's Maxwell House and I don't suspect you keep anything as pedestrian as that in such a fine home."

"I'm not sure what kind of coffee my parents have, to be honest."

"Don't bother checking, dear. You all need to worry about this artwork. I may just have a peek-a-boo at those chocolates though."

Samantha bustled over to the box of Godivas and hovered over it—a vulture sizing up its spoils. She slowly lifted the lid and lowered herself into a suede loveseat, presumably to get a closer look at the offerings.

"Mr. Zieler, what happens next?" Cam asked.

"You're asking me?" Emil scoffed. "I appraise art. I'm not a detective."

Cam looked at Ashlie who snapped a burst of smart phone photos of the framed imposter above the fireplace. "This is going to make for one terrific story," she said.

"Don't you think your parents would prefer to keep this quiet?" Cam asked.

Ashlie shoved the phone into the back pocket of her jeans. She turned to Cam and touched a forefinger to her lips. "I don't know. They're very supportive of my career aspirations. Let me give them a call before ringing the police. Because once we do that, I lose control." She looked at Emil. "Mr. Zieler, would you mind if I interviewed you on video, so that I have something to take to CBC?"

***

"Her parents agreed," Cam said to Kacey. He had returned to Rusted Bonnet to provide the police with a statement about the Galaxes while Ashlie phoned her parents, who had been brunching at a friend's home.

"I know. The chief out in Windsor called Bernie. Apparently, this *Captain* marched into police headquarters berating everyone in his path."

"Full of vim and vinegar?"

"Ha, ha." Kacey shook her head. "That's not even a mixed metaphor."

"Vim and vinegar don't mix?"

Kacey snickered. "As soon as the Windsor chief looped in Bernie, he and a junior officer arrested Gannon and Kamila and seized the Roulands in their attic." She led Cam from an interview room to the police station lobby. Hope was nowhere to be seen.

"I wouldn't be surprised if Bernie's asked for a statement by the press," Cam said. "I imagine Ashlie's pitched the story to the Canadian news by now. She has a good video of the art appraiser and convinced Samantha to recite the story of how she discovered the paintings in the attic." Samantha had deftly steered clear of any mention that Peachy Kleen had been instructed to avoid the area.

"I'm surprised Samantha agreed to be taped."

Cam smiled. "She ate it up. Probably because it gave her a chance to tell the world how clever her son Oliver is. Though she insisted on taking the time to 'get her hair right,' before Ashlie was allowed to hit record."

A stiff wind caught Cam on the back of his neck. He turned toward the door as it slammed. Mitzy strode in on four-inch heels, a fur stole wrapped about her shoulders. "You must arrest my no-good brother-in-law!" she shouted at Kacey. "The brute stole all of my money!"

Kacey's eyes bugged out. "Your brother-in-law?"

"He arrived from Azerbaijan last night."

"Would you like to file a formal report of theft?"

"Definitely. Is it theft if Samir gave him my money or something else?"

Cam rolled his eyes.

"Why don't you tell me what happened," Kacey said coolly. "Let's go into one of the interview rooms."

"I would rather tell you *and Cam* over a Bloody Mary."

"No can do," Kacey said.

"Ack!" Mitzy threw her hands in the air. "My money is almost all gone. Three hundred and fifteen thousand. I tell Cam last night."

Kacey shot a glance in Cam's direction but stayed silent.

"When my brother-in-law shows up at the doorstep from Baku, I had drunk too much to question what he really wanted. But not this morning." She wagged a finger. "I tell him to go away; Samir had no money for him. He said Samir always had money, had been sending it to him for years. Years! Every month. That is where the reverse mortgage payouts went, no doubt."

"What was Jalil using the money for?" Kacey asked.

"Some new trick Samir cooked up. He gave Jalil cash to bribe government workers. You go to jail right away for bribes here. Not in Baku. I do not know the details, but Jalil says it did not work out so well. They did not make money and got themselves in trouble with the mafia in Zaqatala. That is in the north, between Georgia and Dagestan. I cannot believe Samir would trust Jalil to do anything!"

"What kind of trouble were they in with the mafia?" Kacey asked, scribbling furiously in a notebook she'd poached from Hope's desk.

"I do not know. Jalil does not tell me. Most mafia in Azerbaijan deal in heroin or weapons. But that is why Samir sold the home to de Winter. He needed money to pay off the mafia so they do not kill Jalil. Or *my* mother or sisters, says Jalil."

"Do you think the Azerbaijani mafia could have killed Samir?" Kacey asked.

Mitzy pulled her stole tight around her neck. "I never thought of that. Perhaps it is possible."

"Jalil told me last night that he was looking for Samir's lawyer," Cam said. "He said Samir promised him more money."

Kacey stared at Cam.

"I was at Mitzy's when he showed up," Cam explained.

"He said the same to me this morning," Mitzy said. "I tell him there is no money left. Twelve thousand is not enough for me to live on for even one year. I kicked him out."

"How much longer will you be there?" Cam asked.

"Two weeks I think," Mitzy said with a sigh. "Then I turn it over to Mr. de Winter the third. There is no fight left in me. I will use what money I have to fly to Baku. But my lawyer tells me to make certain police are okay with me leaving." She looked at Kacey. "So, is that okay?"

"Let me talk to the chief," Kacey said. "And it doesn't sound like you can legitimately claim theft. If the property was in Samir's and Markuss's names only, it was theirs to sell. And to do whatever they wanted with the proceeds."

"I was afraid of that," Mitzy replied. "Nothing was ever in my name. Stupid me."

"Where is Jalil now?" Kacey asked. "I'd like to speak with him. If Samir had ties to the Azerbaijani mafia, that puts his murder into a whole 'nother place. I may have to call in the feds."

"I do not know where he went. He left the funeral home one hour ago."

***

"Your mother's worried about you," Cam said to Becka as they drove to a pawn shop Cam had frequented months earlier when looking into the death of an au pair.

Becka sighed. "I'm well aware. She thinks I'm being greedy."

"I didn't get that sense," Cam said and accelerated through a yellow light. "I think her concern is that you'll spend more than you have."

"I'll be fine," Becka huffed. "Thank you for taking me here," she added more softly. "I didn't feel comfortable coming alone. Both my mom and Missy thought you'd make me feel safer in a pawn shop than either of them."

Cam parked his Malibu on the curb in front of Grady's Pawn in Madison Heights. A rusted chain link fence surrounded the property and a window touted "Guns" and "Jewelry" in neon pink.

Cam pushed through a heavy door and saw a young man he'd met months earlier named Lucky Moncrief behind the counter.

"Aw, Shih Tzu, not you again," Lucky said when he spotted Cam.

"What's wrong with me?" Cam asked with a grin and stepped forward.

"I thought this guy liked you?" Becka whispered in his ear.

"He did when I slipped him a couple of twenties," Cam whispered back.

"At least you had the decency to bring some *scenery*," Lucky said, his eyes feasting on Becka.

"Stand down," Cam said. "She's taken."

"And I don't take kindly to being called scenery," Becka said, then added, "Is that a *Thriller* jacket?" Lucky was wearing a red leather—or, possibly, vinyl—jacket with a large black "V" in the front.

"Michael's my man," Lucky said. He looked at Cam. "Last time you was here, cops got up in my grill."

"You had valuable information related to a crime."

"I s'pose. You got more questions 'bout something?"

"When I was in here before, you told me about a Cash-for-

Gold place. I was wondering if you'd recommend it as a place to sell silver."

"That'd be Johnny Chiu's place. Him and boss man are friendly. But no need to go all the way to Eleven Mile. I can buy the stuff here."

"It's worth a lot," Cam said.

"Bring it in and let's have a look. I'll call Grady—boss man here—if we need to break out the big bucks."

Cam paced out to his car and popped the trunk while Becka waited inside with Lucky. The three silver bars lay under a light blanket. Cam squared his back to ward off any curious passersby—not that he saw anyone on the street—and heaved a bar into a duffel bag. He set the bag between his feet, re-covered the other bars, and pressed the trunk shut.

Becka was perusing a jewelry case next to the counter when Cam reentered the shop. "What do you think of these?" she asked as he hoisted the duffel onto the countertop. She pointed at a set of purplish square stone earrings.

"I can give you a terrific price on those," Lucky said. "They're just about perfect quality. Run you three grand at a luxury place."

"This isn't luxury?" Cam joked.

"Man, don't diss this joint. Fine quality goods is what we've got. Just none of the snooty attitude."

"Or unstained carpet," Becka quipped. "Kidding," she said and put her hands up playfully.

"How 'bout we do s'more kidding at my place?" Lucky said to Becka. "Say nine o'clock tonight. Iss' just around the corner from here."

"No thank you," Becka said.

"All right then," Lucky said. "Your boy here said you was taken. But I figured that wass' just wishful thinkin' on his part."

"How about we take a look at the silver?" Cam said.

"Right," Lucky said and unzipped the duffel bag. "Sweet mother of pearl, man!"

"We have two more of the same size," Becka said.

"Well, then triple mother of pearl! Hold on," Lucky said and ran around the counter to the front door. He locked it with a set of keys dangling from a belt loop on a bungee cord and flipped a sign in the window from "open" to "closed."

"Lemme lock the back door and call Grady. This ain't your momma's silver rosary."

***

Grady Jones—proprietor of Grady's Pawn—was not at all who Cam expected. Fifteen minutes after Lucky phoned him, a pale-skinned redhead came into the showroom through the back door. A pink blemish the size of a gumdrop protruded from his neck.

"Pleased to meet you," he said to Cam and Becka in an Irish accent. "Lucky tells me you have three silver bars the size of Texas."

"Something like that," Cam said. "I weighed them. We've got a 65 pounder, 67, and 68. The one in the duffel is the 65. The other two are still in my trunk."

Grady opened the bag and hefted the bar onto the countertop. "What's their origin?"

"A shipwreck," Becka said quickly. "My father was a welder in South Africa. The bars were recovered by a dive crew."

"And they're pure silver?"

"That's what he said. He gave them to me after he passed away."

"Do you have documentation?"

"I have letters from my father. No one's contesting that they belong to me."

"I mean do you have any paperwork on bars themselves?"

"No," Becka said. "Do I need any?"

"Not necessarily," Grady replied. "But before I can quote you a price, without papers from a reputable shop, I'll need to test the bars for purity myself."

"Of course," Becka said.

"The best way to test for pure silver is by X-Ray fluorescence—XRF. My friend Johnny has an XRF analyzer. It's an amazing thing, looks like a computerized drill gun. You press the end against a piece of metal, pull the trigger to activate it, and within a matter of seconds, you get a digital readout of the metals inside—down to the precise percentage."

"That sounds perfect," Cam said.

"It would be, only Johnny's in Tijuana. He took his teenage son there on vacation." Grady laughed. "As if raising the kid in a Cash-for-Gold shop ain't seedy enough!"

"Man, why you always playing down our joints," Lucky said. "Iss' nice enough here for me."

"It is for me, too," Grady said. "But Johnny's place needs twice as many bars on the windows as we do here. Lots of hoods down in that 'hood."

"Whatever," Lucky said.

"Anyway," Grady said turning his attention back to Cam and Becka, "the XRF analyzers run several thousand bucks, and that's for a used one off of eBay. I don't do enough in metals to justify it. But an acid test will do the trick."

"Can we do that here?" Becka asked.

"Absolutely," Grady said. "Only as long as you don't mind if I file down a little into the bar. Otherwise, we can wait a few days for Johnny to get back."

"As long as it doesn't hurt the value," Becka said.

"It won't," Grady said. "Seeing as how whoever buys it is just going to melt it down."

"What's the filing for?" Cam asked.

"Lots of bars are plated so it's best to test under the surface. Now, I don't know about ones this old coming from wherever came it was from."

"Sri Lanka," Becka said.

"Okay, I have no idea when and where plating came into practice, but nowadays there's silver and gold plating on pretty much everything."

"But that's mostly jewelry, right?" Cam asked. "Why would anyone plate a bar?"

"As a ruse," Grady said. "Not that you don't look on the up-and-up, but I don't mess around."

"I don't blame you," Cam said.

"There are acid test kits you can buy online. That's what I'm going to use. If the person being duped isn't the brightest, the con man drops a bit of acid on a bar, it shows positive for silver and—voila—the mark thinks the bar is silver. That's because the acid never penetrates the plating. So, what I usually do is file down a little line."

"Do you need all three bars?" Becka asked.

"Let me start with this one. Lucky, can you grab the silver file?"

Lucky disappeared into a side room and emerged seconds later with a shaft of stiff gray metal, the letter "S" marked on its small wooden handle. He handed it to Grady.

"I have a workbench back here," Grady said and retreated toward the rear of the showroom. "Bring the bar."

Cam lifted it and followed Grady, with Becka and Lucky trailing.

Cam parked the silver bar on the bench and stepped to the side. Grady sawed into a top edge of the bar with the file, cutting a thin line a half inch long and a millimeter or two deep.

Seemingly satisfied, he pulled back a workbench drawer and

removed a small dropper bottle. Reddish brown liquid sloshed inside the clear plastic. "This is a mix of nitric and muriatic acids," Grady explained. "I'll add a couple of drops. If it stays opaque and reddish-brown after about ten seconds, you've got yourself the real deal. Anything less than pure silver will cause it to turn a clear greenish-blue."

"What if its part silver and part something else?" Cam asked.

"If it's an alloy like that, we'll see something in between," Grady said. He stretched latex gloves over thick fingers and slid a pair of safety glasses that had been perched on his forehead over his eyes. "Stand back. The smallest bit of splatter could blind you," he warned.

All three observers took a pace back. Grady unscrewed the dropper lid from then bottle, squeezed liquid into the narrow dropper tube, then centered its tip over the bar's file mark. He released two drops squarely into the crevice. They filled the tiny space and the overflow pooled into a tiny puddle on the bar's surface.

Cam stepped forward to get a better look. Within seconds, the brownish-red liquid—both in the crevice and on the surface—morphed into a translucent turquoise.

***

"What movie did you see?" Cam asked. He had dropped off a disappointed Becka and the three bars back at her basement apartment and an afternoon housekeeping job had left him within ten minutes of the flat Shane and Jelly Roll shared.

Shane rubbed a palm against his untrimmed facial hair. Sprigs of brown and gray scattered haphazardly like thatches of bean sprouts. "The new Bond flick. It was pretty good."

"Did Markuss enjoy it, too?"

"Why are you asking me about the movie? You ain't a cop."

Shane wore a black Detroit Pistons muscle shirt, baggy athletic shorts, and dingy tube socks. He flung a dart at a board hanging on unpainted drywall in the kitchen-cum-family room.

"Because something stinks and I don't mean your socks. Did you know your uncle's in town?"

"Uncle?" Shane slung another dart. It drilled the triple-twenty space.

"Jalil. He flew in from Azerbaijan."

Shane didn't flinch. He tossed a third dart then strode to the board and plucked out the group.

"That doesn't surprise you?" Cam asked.

"I only met him once. I was pretty young."

"He hasn't gotten in touch with you?"

"No." Shane picked up a beer can. "I wonder what he wants."

"Mainly to talk with your father's lawyer," Cam said.

Shane funneled beer down his throat, seemingly without swallowing. "Won't do him no good. Mom says there's nothing left. She's going back to Baku, you know."

"I heard." Cam leaned against a wall opposite the dart board. Shane hadn't invited him to sit. "Did your father have ties to the mafia in Azerbaijan?"

Shane shrugged his shoulders. He set his beer in between a television and a gaming system console on a rolling cart. "I have no idea. It wouldn't surprise me."

"How about Markuss? Might he have a connection?"

"Markuss?" Shane snorted. He chucked a dart at the board. "You must be kidding. Can you imagine that old man in a sharkskin suit?"

"I was surprised you went to the movies with him."

"You're back on that." Shane scratched the tail of a dart against his cheek. "I didn't want to lug furniture that night—guy who lived here asked me an' Jelly to help him. So, when the old man offered me a ticket, I took it."

Cam's mind sprang to the forgotten wallet. "How did he pay for it?"

"What do'ya mean?"

"Did he pull a credit card out of his wallet or did he have cash in his pocket?"

"Is this how you helped the police solve that murder last fall —by asking a bunch of dumb ass questions?" He whipped a dart at the board—a bullseye. "I have no clue how the dude paid. He handed me a ticket in the morning. Told me to meet him there."

Cam pushed himself away from the wall. "He gave you the ticket in the morning?"

"Yup. Said he and the missus had gone to see a show the night before so he just picked 'em up then. I guess his wife changed her mind and decided seeing Daniel Craig without a shirt wasn't worth two hours of her time."

"And you were free?"

"On a Monday night, sure. I asked if he was buying snacks, too, and he gave me a twenty on the spot."

"What time was the show?" Cam shoved his hands in his jeans pockets.

"Eight o'clock. I almost skipped it because of the snow, but a free ticket's a free ticket. Plus, if Jelly saw me here, I'd have been hauling boxes for Crater." Shane picked up his beer, drained it, and crushed the can in his fist.

Smack around the time of the murder, Cam thought. "And you and Markuss were together for the whole movie?"

Shane pinched skin on his neck. "Yes and no."

"What do you mean?" Cam cracked his knuckles.

"I sat toward the front. Markuss was in the back. He couldn't find me."

Cam's eyes bulged. "Wait. You didn't actually see Markuss

at the theater?"

Shane shook his head. "No, I saw him all right." He plodded to the refrigerator and plucked out another beer. He didn't offer one to Cam.

"I'm confused," Cam said.

"And I'm confused as to why you give a shit."

"Because the chief hasn't ruled me out as a suspect," Cam said flatly.

"You?" Shane laughed. "Don't think a momma's boy like you could stab anybody."

Cam let the jab slide.

"So, you come here asking questions because you think I did it?" Shane eyes were vacant.

"I just want to know where everybody who worked at Paul Bearer's was that night."

Shane shrugged. "Doesn't matter to me. I didn't kill no one and I'm screwed anyway seeing as how mom doesn't own the home. Need a driver for those cleaning vans of yours?"

Cam shook his head.

"I figured not," Shane said.

"Can we get back to the theater?" Cam asked.

Shane flopped into a worn corduroy-covered chair. "I got to the movies a few minutes before eight, but Markuss wasn't there yet," he explained. "Got myself a chili dog and some Sour Patch Kids, then grabbed a seat. I had to turn my phone off, you know. When the show ended and I powered up, there was a text from Markuss."

"When did he send it?" Cam asked.

"Around a quarter after eight."

"What did it say?"

Shane scratched his forearm with a dart, then filled the silence. "It's no big secret—just that he couldn't find me in the dark. Said he'd take me for a burger."

"Is that what happened?"

"Yep. I saw him in the second to last row as soon as the lights came on. We got burgers and shakes at Knapp's and that was that." Shane popped the top on his Busch Light.

"Did you tell the police?"

"They didn't ask me anything that specific. I just told the deputy about seeing the show."

"Did you talk about the movie when you went for burgers?"

"Of course. What else would we talk about?"

"I have no idea." Cam looked down at his shoes. "Did you happen to notice whether he pulled out a wallet when he paid for the burgers?"

"He said he left it at Paul Bearer's. I guess he didn't notice until the check came. It wasn't a problem—he had a spare fifty in his car."

Chapter 20

"What do you think, Bait?" Cam mashed a foam stress ball in his fist, then unclenched and let it fall to the dining room floor. "Did Markuss sit in the back of a movie theater by himself for an hour and a half or was he using Shane as a cover?"

Bait circled a treasure chest.

"Markuss goes to the movies on Sunday and picks up a pair of tickets to the next night's show. Maybe he was there with his wife and tells her he wants to see the Bond movie. She says, 'no way,' so they see a romantic comedy. Or a blood and guts horror flick for all I know. But he gets a ticket for the following evening. Two tickets. The next morning, he asks Shane to join him. Why Shane? I'm pretty sure Markuss didn't think highly of him."

Cam mimicked Bait's pattern and paced in a circle around the dining room table. "Precisely because Shane isn't too bright? Because Shane would believe, based on a text that could've been sent from anywhere, that Markuss was in the back of the theater the entire time? But if Markuss wasn't at the movies, what was doing? Robbing Mrs. Bitter's body and stabbing Samir? That doesn't make sense because Markuss was stabbed when he went back to get his wallet, hours after Samir died." Cam grunted. "That points to Mitzy, of course."

Cam shook flakes into the fish tank. Bait bolted toward them.

A cymbal-clanging crescendo crashed into Cam's skull. *What if Markuss was telling the truth in his text and Shane was lying?* To Bait, he said, "Markuss shows up to the movies a few minutes late and can't locate Shane because *he* isn't there. He's at Paul Bearer's killing dear old daddy. Then *Shane* jets back in time to slip into the theater before the film ends. After the movie, he and Markuss go for burgers. And maybe Markuss asks about the movie, just casual banter. Only Shane can't speak about it because he didn't see it. When Markuss tells him he has to go back to the funeral home to pick up his wallet, Shane realizes that Markuss will see Samir's body and put two-and-two together, so he follows Markuss and attacks him."

Bait silently munched flakes.

"But if that were the case, wouldn't Markuss have told the police that Shane seemed confused about the movie?" Cam recommenced pacing. "One other thing's strange. Markuss told me he didn't realize his wallet was missing until just before he went to bed, not at a burger joint."

***

"What's it to you that I'm getting a little Mrs. Robinson?" Chet demanded.

He stood on Cam's porch, fists clenched, his chin jutting toward Cam. The bell had rung just as Cam finished cleaning Bait's tank.

"Shouldn't you be in Chicago?"

"I should," Chet growled. "Only I hear you've been asking a

lot of questions about me and I need to set you straight."

Who did he hear it from? Mitzy? Cam wondered. "Set me straight how?" he asked. He noticed a small symbol tattooed on the underside of one of Chet's forearms—slashes of ink in an undecipherable pattern. The sleeves on Chet's sweater were pushed to his elbows. Cam had no idea what it meant. Only that it didn't jibe with Chet's preppy persona.

"It's simple," Chet said. "I slept with Mitzy when I was eighteen. Older woman, still pretty hot. She taught me a few things. Trust me, they've served me well."

"And you stayed in touch after you went off to school?" Cam asked. He was standing in his doorframe, nervous that Chet might punch him, but not fearing much else in the broad daylight.

"Of course not." Chet laughed. "What do I need with a woman two decades older than me, hundreds of miles away. I do quite well in Chicago."

"So, you didn't sleep with her a few nights ago?"

Chet took a step closer to Cam. His breath smelled of meat. "That's none of your business." He jabbed a finger into Cam's chest. "I only give one warning and this is it. Back off. If I have to come back to Rusted Bonnet again, I'm not coming alone and you won't be happy."

***

A knock came just after four in the afternoon. Cam welcomed the distraction from his slog through timesheets, payroll, and sundry client requests for scheduling changes. Feeling the need to escape from his home and Chet's threat, Cam had fled to the confines of Peachy Kleen. On the doorstep, Geoffrey Rampart's cinnamon skin and whiskey-colored eyes complemented one another in the afternoon sun.

"Tell me *the Observer* is looking for a new cleaning crew," Cam said by way of greeting.

The reporter shook his head. "Can I talk to you for a few minutes? Before the onslaught hits."

"Onslaught?" Cam took a step backward and waived Geoffrey inside the otherwise empty office space.

The older man stepped onto a rubber mat and pulled off a pair of woolen gloves. "The police arrested Blair Lamb and it's bloody red hot. A woman who looks that good drugging men and selling their house keys. It's a slam dunk to be the lead everywhere. Word is ABC and CBS crews are on their way from Detroit. Right now. They'll want to get a story for the six o'clock news."

Cam swallowed hard. "How did you know I was involved?"

"Arrest records are open to the public, unless they're part of an ongoing investigation. But even then, you know how fast word travels around the village. And a juicy story has its way of making it to the news stations. Not from me, of course."

"So, is it safe to assume you want to break the story?"

Geoffrey held out his palms. "Yes, but I'm offering to let you dictate its direction. If we hurry, I can get it online before the six o'clock news. That way, *you* have the chance to set the tone."

Cam glanced at his watch. He'd been scheduled to clean a 1920s brick Colonial on the west end of town. "Just give me two minutes to see if Tabby will work overtime."

***

Cam watched the six o'clock news from the comfort of his sofa, wearing nothing but boxers and a frayed T-shirt with the heat cranked up to seventy-five and a pint of MC2 in his lap— mint chocolate chip.

The CBS local news kicked off its coverage with split screen shots of Blair—to the left, a yearbook photo of a breathtaking senior, to the right, a mugshot. Even in the latter, a wave of hair tumbling over one eye and high cheekbones captured her natural beauty.

"Blair Lamb of Rusted Bonnet has been arrested in connection with a devious plot to dupe scores of metro area men," the newscaster began. "Only this scheme is more twisted than meets the eye." The television man's own baby blues glimmered. "The twenty-eight-year-old cosmetologist is accused of picking up wealthy gents in area hotspots, drugging them, and taking them back to their homes. She leaves the men unconscious, only to wake in the morning stripped down to their underwear with a foggy memory of an attractive brunette. This is no one-night stand, but they're taken advantage of all right. According to unnamed sources, Lamb watches her mark type in his security code and steals a set of keys after the man passes out, only to return them after a copy is made. And months later, the home is burglarized. A man by the name of Devon Schuler is currently being sought by Bay City police as a person of interest in connection with the crime spree."

An artist's pencil rendition of the burglar flashed onto the television screen—Pee-wee Herman sporting a ribbed muscle shirt and ear gauges. Cam exhaled. He whispered a silent prayer for the story to end there.

It didn't. The newscaster's face reappeared on screen. "The roofies to riches scam was unearthed by a man from Lamb's home town. Cameron Reddick, the comely con artist's final victim, declined to comment."

"Arrgh!" Cam screamed. After providing an explanation of his experience to Geoffrey—who had agreed to keep his name out of his story—Cam had rushed home, locked his front door, and refused to answer the persistent knocks and phone calls that figuratively rattled his townhouse.

He stood and stomped toward Bait as the screen flickered to a commercial hyping Buick as a luxury car brand—it wasn't fooling anyone. "At least they didn't find a picture of me," he said to the goldfish.

Cam turned back, aimed the remote control at the television, and flipped through the news channels. He didn't hear his name mentioned again. "Maybe it won't be so bad," Cam said to Bait. "How many people around here watch CBS news at six?" He looked at his fish. "Don't answer that."

"What do you think about Blair as Samir's killer?" Cam said out loud. His mind flashed to the angle of the knife protruding from Samir's back. Blair was several inches shorter than Samir —so the upward slant fit. Plus, she didn't have an alibi for the night he was murdered. Of course, Cam hadn't pinpointed a motive for her either. *Unless Samir uncovered the roofie scam and threatened to expose her.*

As for the others, Mitzy's alibi was non-existent and Cam could punch holes in Shane's. Even if the human Crater confirmed Jelly Roll's story, what did that prove? Jelly could've slipped him a couple of hundreds to spin the police a yarn about moving furniture. In the middle of a snow storm no less. Piper was conveniently occupied at eight o'clock as well, telephoning a friend. Had she timed the call to throw off the police? But how would she know to go back to the funeral home closer to eleven to attack Markuss?

Cam slapped a hand against his forehead. For the longest time, he had assumed that the killer intended to take out one man. Either Samir or Markuss. But what if there was a link that prompted the murderer to go after both, *independently*?

Had Mitzy discovered the partnership in advance of Jackson de Winter showing up at Paul Bearer's with a crane? If so, she deserved an Oscar.

A rapping at his door interrupted Cam's thoughts. Annoyed

by the persistence of the press, he shouted, "I have no comment!" from the sofa.

"Cam, it's me," Kacey's voice came through the door. "Piper Quick's been arrested for Samir's murder."

Chapter 21

"You're yanking my leg, right?" Cam asked as soon as he opened the door.

"I'm not," Kacey said, then pulled off a glove with her teeth.

"Wow. Is Emma with my mother?"

"She is. I tried calling, but you didn't pick up. I can understand why."

"I turned off the phone," Cam said. He led Kacey into the kitchen. "Have you eaten dinner? I was just going to nuke some frozen Indian."

"Darby was kind enough to make dinner for Emma and me. Not that I had time to eat it there—I wolfed down one of her falafel pitas on the drive over here."

"Those are my favorite. Do you mind if I eat? I'm famished." Cam popped open the freezer and selected lamb vindaloo.

"Of course not. How are you holding up? I saw the news."

Cam freed the lamb from its cardboard pen and pierced the plastic cover with a fork. "I'll live." He shoved the container into the microwave. "Did Piper kill Samir?"

"Bernie certainly thinks so," Kacey said. "I found the boning knife a few hours ago and Piper's fingerprints were the only ones on it. I went back to her place—the knife is part of a matching set from her kitchen."

"That's pretty incriminating."

"Maybe," Kacey's voice was low.

"Where did you find it?"

"On the side lawn at Paul Bearer's. The snow finally melted enough for me to scour the grounds. There's dried blood on it. We'll confirm that it matches Markuss's."

"You had Piper's prints on file?"

"We took them from everyone who worked at Paul Bearer's. Besides, Piper's were in a military database. She did a stint with the Coast Guard."

"So, Piper Quick's her real name?"

"Actually, Piper's her middle name," Kacey said. "Her first name is Danica. Much nicer than Piper if you ask me."

The microwave beeped.

Cam retrieved his dinner. "What did she have to say for herself?"

"Not much. She asked for a lawyer straight away so we haven't interviewed her yet. Of course, that didn't stop Bernie from blurting out that we found her boning knife."

"Did she respond to that?"

"She said, 'I knew something didn't seem right.'" Kacey, sitting on a kitchen stool, slid a foot under her backside.

Cam leaned across the other side of the counter and raised a spoonful of lamb to his lips. He blew on it gently. "Any idea what she meant?"

"It made me wonder if her home had been broken into." Kacey said.

Cam's brain lurched. "Blair?" He set the spoon back into the plastic tray to let the meat cool. "She's friendly with at least one burglar and lives two doors down from Piper."

"The thought definitely crossed my mind." Kacey inspected her nails—a clawed-at cuticle had begun to scab. "Cam, why would she drop the knife in the snow right next to the funeral home?"

"Someone was chasing her?" Cam postulated.

"Who? If someone saw her kill Samir, they would've come forward. Besides, Samir had a diving knife in his back. The boning knife I found was used on Markuss three hours later."

"So, if Piper isn't the murderer, why are hers the only prints on it?"

"Because it's her knife and the killer was careful. He wore gloves when he swiped it from her kitchen and attacked Markuss."

Cam spooned vindaloo into his mouth, savoring its zing.

"Which would mean there was premeditation," Kacey added. "But I'm still getting stuck on the timing. If someone took a knife from Piper's kitchen to frame her, why not stab Samir with it?"

"Did the diving knife have any prints on it?"

"Unfortunately not."

"So, the killer stabs Samir with the diving knife, careful to keep his prints off of it. But he gets scared and decides to frame Piper."

"So Markuss is attacked to set her up."

"Exactly. The killer sneaks into Piper's townhouse and grabs a knife from the kitchen."

Kacey shook her head. "That doesn't work. Piper said she was at home on the telephone, then stayed in for the rest of the evening. Plus, how would the killer know Markuss was coming back to the funeral home to pick up his wallet?"

"Shane knew." Cam cracked his neck.

"Don't do that! It scares the bejeezus out of me."

"Sorry." He filled her in on Shane's story about not sitting with Markuss at the theater.

"What?" Kacey shouted. "I can't believe I didn't get that out of either one of them."

"I got lucky," Cam said. "By the time Markuss went to pay for their burgers, Shane knew he left his wallet at the funeral home. He could've called Jelly Roll when Markuss went to find his emergency cash in the car."

"Fascinating. Markuss invites Shane to a movie, they go in a snowstorm, and don't even sit together. Truth is stranger than fiction, but that's a parade of oddities right there." Kacey blew into her hands. "Let's say Shane and Jelly Roll *are* working together. Shane kills Samir using the movies as an alibi, which is why Markuss can't find him in the theater until after the show. Then Shane freaks out when Markuss tells him he's headed back to Paul Bearer's after their burgers so he calls or texts Jelly and asks him to swipe a knife from Piper's house. Maybe he got lucky and Piper was already asleep or in the shower or something. Then Jelly attacks Markuss, only he can't do anything right, including kill a man."

"But why kill Markuss? Samir's dead. They figure Mitzy will give them run of the shop."

"Either Shane panicked and thought Markuss would realize he stabbed Samir because he couldn't find him in the theater or they knew that Samir and Markuss were partners," Kacey said. "But didn't know they had sold the place to de Winter."

"It's not perfect, but not bad." Cam swallowed another bite of his meal. "The hardest thing for me to get my head around is the fact that *Markuss* invited Shane to the theater. That doesn't make sense with Shane and Jelly as the bad guys."

Kacey grunted. "Good point."

"How about this: the killer's only target was Samir. At least initially. He kills Samir, then panics and decides to frame Piper like we said. So, he steals her knife and lies in wait to attack the next person to enter Paul Bearer's. It just happened to be Markuss but it could've just as easily been Mitzy coming downstairs or the first person to arrive in the morning."

"But Piper was usually the first to arrive in the morning. It wouldn't be too bright to frame the person you're most likely to attack."

Cam shrugged. "Stupidity is a growth industry."

"I'm worried that Bernie had an ulterior motive in arresting Piper," Kacey said. "Subconsciously, of course."

"Being?"

"With Piper in the crosshairs, he has an excuse not to call in the FBI."

"He's equipped to tackle the mafia by himself?" Cam laughed.

"Just the opposite. He's completely ignoring the possibility."

"He doesn't want to rock the apple cart."

Kacey sniggered. "Exactly. I haven't seen anyone in the village who sticks out. Of course, modern day mobsters probably don't."

"And are you comfortable holding Piper in a cell?"

"For now, yes. Piper would have to be crazy to leave the weapon right on the Paul Bearer property, but it did have her prints on it."

"Any chance she left it there for that very reason?"

"To throw us off because we know she's no dummy?"

Cam nodded.

"It crossed my mind. Still, I don't have a good motive for Piper to want Samir dead."

"It's possible Samir fooled around with Piper, though I'm not sure."

"I bet he tried," Kacey said.

"And Mitzy told me Piper wanted a raise."

"Who doesn't?" Kacey paused. "I haven't asked you why you've been spending so much time with Mitzy.... I know it's none of my business."

Cam held up his hands. "It is your business because my only interest is finding Samir's killer." He looked Kacey in the eyes. "Mitzy did make a pass at me last night before Jalil arrived, but I brushed her off."

Kacey broke their mutual stare. "I shouldn't have asked," she said weakly. "By the way, I thought you'd like to know that we couldn't find anyone who had a security camera near Edith Smithwick's house."

"The woman who found Mrs. Bitter's necklace?"

Kacey nodded, then crinkled her nose. "She smelled. Like leftover scallops and ranch dressing. Whoever dumped the necklace would leap to the top of the suspect list. And if it was Piper, that would've been a nail in the coffin."

"I suppose. Have you spoken with Jalil?"

Kacey rose from her stool. "Not yet. He seems to have disappeared."

Chapter 22

"It might not be the worst idea for you to take a couple of days off and head out of town." Nestled in a corner of Cam's leather sectional, Darby swirled a glass of a red blend. A fleck of fire popped and a glowing ember caught in the iron-finished screen fronting the fireplace. She looked at Cam who was seated at one end of the sectional. "Until the reporters stop banging down your door. Here and at work. Have you told the girls about what happened with Blair?"

The 'girls,' being his cleaning staff, three of whom were older than Cam. "I texted and asked them not to comment if anyone from the media tried to question them."

"That was smart." Darby sipped her wine. After a moment, she added, "So were you and Blair on a date?"

Cam saw right through his mother's question. He knew she wanted him to get back together with Kacey. At least, eventually. Not only for Emma's sake, but also because Darby genuinely liked Kacey. Loved her, in fact.

"I was at the Stagger, just for a late dinner," Cam said. "She approached me."

"Are you on any of the dating websites?"

"I've looked at a couple, but haven't set up a profile. I'm still trying to get adjusted here."

Darby smiled at him. Her teeth shone white in the firelight. "Well, you're doing a very good job of that."

***

"Lead weights? I don't understand. Why would a ship be transporting lead weights?" Missy asked.

She, Becka, Malika, and Cam were in the Peachy Kleen bullpen on Zoom with a Mr. Dominic Ellum—a retired hull repairman from South Africa.

After Grady Jones—the pawn shop owner—had declared the bars to be made of lead rather than silver, Becka had scoured the Internet and microfiche at the Detroit public library for any mention of the Jaffna Clipper recovery efforts. She expected to find scores of archived articles, but only unearthed a single op-ed from a paper in Durbin, South Africa. It was penned by Mr. D. Ellum and railed against a co-worker and two other men for bilking him out of his life savings.

Becka had located Ellum through social media and now his aquiline nose twitched on Missy's laptop screen.

"There never was a dive," Ellum said in response to Missy's question. "They never even found the Clipper." His weather-beaten face was the color of clean smoke. "Jared Nix. He was a good ten years younger than me or Gak. He was one of the odd jobs men. Not a skilled worker like us. Scraped barnacles, painted rails, did whatever grunt work needed doing. One morning maybe six weeks into the *Destiny* project, Nix comes onto the deck looking like the goose that laid the golden egg. Couldn't wipe the smile off of his face. He tells some of the guys that he and two of his buddies are expert divers and had been looking for the Jaffna Clipper for months. Every day on their days off. Told us the Clipper's story and how legend had it that the ship transported loads of silver. Claimed that under maritime law, whoever brought up its treasure was the rightful owner."

Ellum coughed then took a drag from a cigarette. "Most of the guys laughed him off as a teller of tall tales, but some of us were interested, including Gak and me. We didn't dismiss him. For me it was the look in his eyes. Son-of-a-gun must be the best liar I've ever seen. How someone could fake a look like that I'll never know. After work, he led a group of us—twelve in all—back to his apartment and showed us a bar. It looked ancient. Water weary, gray, just what I'd expect if silver sat in salt water for over hundred years. He said it was the smallest of a huge stack of bars that were down there—it was the only thing they could carry back without equipment. And the equipment cost money. Money the three divers didn't have. He had a chunk of old twisted metal, too. It was so corroded you could just barely make out J-blank-F-F-blank-A. It sure looked like an authentic piece of scrap from a ship named the Jaffna Clipper."

"He made it himself?" Cam asked.

"He must have. Either Nix or one of his cohorts. His two mates were at the apartment. They looked like sturdy men and talked the talk of folks who knew the sea. One of the men said his father was an attorney and he'd drafted up contracts for a stake in the haul for any of us who were willing to part with 35,000 Rand. That's worth about $2,500 American dollars now, a whole lot back then. Not one of us had that kind of money, except for one of the foremen who made more than the rest of us and married a woman from a well-to-do family. So, the rest of us borrowed from our families—parents, siblings, cousins. One guy even borrowed 10,000 Rand from his priest. Ten out of the twelve of us came up with the dough. Myself and Gak included. I raided my retirement account. I don't know where he got the cash. The deal in the contract was that for 35,000 Rand, the ten of us would share 50% of the haul and the three who found the Clipper and made the dive would split the rest."

"Did any of you go with them on the salvage trip?" Becka asked.

"They said no one else was allowed. Even though we were business partners, they couldn't risk letting anyone else know the coordinates of the sunken ship. That wasn't surprising. In Knysna in those days, Nix and his crew would've risked getting their throats cut if someone else knew the location of that much treasure. So, we signed the papers and handed over the money."

"They could've just run off with it," Malika said.

"No," Ellum replied. "The money was held in a safe in an accountant's office until after the salvage."

"That was smart," Cam said. "To make it seem legitimate."

"It was, but what wasn't smart is that none of us had the silver tested before passing the cash to Nix and his friends. Five weeks after we gave them the money, Nix invited the ten of us back to his apartment. He gave us bottles of beer, not cans. A sign of good fortune. He and his friends spun a wild tale about the dive, including a bout of lightning and an encounter with a sizeable squid. It made for good storytelling. Then he led us into his bedroom and yanked a tarp from a mound on the floor. There were exactly sixty bars of silver. Or what the ten of us thought were silver. Ten each for the crew who recovered the treasure and three each for the investors. What a windfall we all said it was—worth ten times the money we put in. I remember thinking how thrilled the priest would be when my co-worker told him."

"No one was suspicious?" Cam asked.

"That it wasn't genuine? Honestly, no. Though one of the investors was wary about the size of the recovery. 'You've shown us sixty bars here,' he said as we stood in Nix's bedroom. 'How do we know your friends don't have more silver in their apartments?' he asked."

"That was a good question," Malika said.

"It was and Nix didn't have an answer for it. Instead, he said all we had was his word. But he insisted that he would not let any of us take our three bars until we released our 35,000 Rand from the accountant's safe. He told the skeptical investor that if he wasn't satisfied with three enormous bars of silver he could take back his investment. The man declined and took the bars."

"Why didn't you tell my father they were fake?" Becka asked.

"Unfortunately, I didn't discover it until a year later," Ellum explained. "And by then I didn't know where Gak was. Nix never returned to the Destiny and no one batted an eye. He was the owner of a fortune in silver, or so we thought. No man that wealthy would ever scrub barnacles again. Obviously, he and his friends had just run off with our cash. They must have purchased sixty lead ingots from a yard for peanuts.

"The man who'd received money from the priest said he had a cousin who wrote for a local newspaper—he wanted to tell his cousin the story of the great Jaffna Clipper salvage. But someone else—I can't remember who after all of these years—warned him off of that idea, because he wasn't certain maritime law worked the way Nix had described it. If the papers found out, he said, the police could take our bars if the descendants of original owners of the silver came forward. We were all too scared to ask a lawyer who might call the police. Better to wait one year then sell the bars in different parts of South Africa. And that's what we did. Only it sounds like Gak kept his for you, Miss."

"He did," Becka said into the laptop screen.

"Well, by the time I tried to sell mine, we had long finished the Destiny and all parted ways. I moved up to Durbin for a job. Anyway, I remember the day I found out those bars weren't silver. Probably the worst day of my life other than the day my mother died. I was so angry. Only I had no one to take the anger out on. Well, Nix and his buddies, sure, but I had no idea where they were. I didn't know where any of the other investors were either, so I wrote the opinion piece you all tracked down. I just needed to vent. But the paper was in Durbin and I can't imagine Gak would've seen it."

"Thank you for telling us," Malika said.

"You're welcome," Ellum said. "It made my blood boil all over again when I heard from you all. But you had a right to know. Besides, it's sort of a relief to tell someone in person. Well, over the Internet at least."

Wednesday, February 17

The Chevy Chase enclave of Washington D.C. reeked of money. Two lawyer families mingled with retired executives living off the fat of bloated government contracts. Bordered by Rock Creek Park on one side and the Maryland neighborhood of the same name on the other, the quiet tree-lined streets were littered with BMW convertibles and Land Rovers.

Cam sat in his Malibu on the curb in front of Ward Porter's manse—a stucco and stone French provincial. A retired New Jersey cop living in a posh neighborhood could mean almost anything, Cam reasoned—it didn't necessarily translate to being on the take. Plus, Cam recalled, Samir had tried to bribe the Cape May police and failed.

Cam had weaseled Porter's name from Hope, the Rusted Bonnet police receptionist. A bit of online digging revealed that the officer who had written the notes on Samir's case sold his home in Cape May three years earlier and moved to Washington

—no more than fifteen miles from Falls Church, where Cam had spent five years finding himself.

As soon as he crossed the Mason-Dixon line, tears had begun to well in his eyes. Not because Cam missed the D.C. environs or even any particular person—he had made few close friends in the area. But because of time lost. Time he could have spent with Kacey, watching Emma grow from an infant to the inquisitive and exuberant girl she had become. Falls Church, Virginia had not seen him develop as an engineer—a degree from a Midwestern state school with scant experience had relegated him to the professional dregs in a city teeming with overachievers. But it *had* helped him realize exactly where his fidelity lay: in the small town of his youth with the family he abandoned.

By the time Cam reached Frederick, Maryland, he was openly sobbing and he'd plowed through an entire box of tissues before he parked in Chevy Chase an hour later. His eyes were bloodshot—leaving Michigan at midnight certainly hadn't helped.

Now, in the midmorning sunlight, staring up at Ward Porter's home, Cam pushed all thoughts of self-reproach to the subterranean of his mind. He cracked open the car door, splashed lukewarm bottled water in his face, and wiped it away with a sweater sleeve. With a photocopy of Officer Porter's notes from the Orucov file in hand, he marched up the flagstone drive and punched the doorbell.

The man who answered the door wore a matching camel-colored T-shirt and linen shorts. With a barrel chest, dark-tanned, meaty thighs, and no neck, he resembled a Christmas goose. But his smile stretched from one crinkled ear to the other.

He extended a hand to Cam. "What are you selling today? Can't be life insurance at my age." A chuckle.

"No sir," Cam said and ran a wobbling hand through his thinning hair. "Are you Ward Porter?"

"In the flesh and blood."

Cam exhaled with relief. "I just spent the night driving in from Michigan to see you. If you have a few minutes, I'd like to ask you about a case you worked on in Cape May."

Porter's eyes narrowed. "You're a reporter then?"

Cam literally took a step backward, his heel clipping the top step. He caught his balance. "No, sir." Cam wondered what had caused Porter's reaction. "A man you investigated years ago was murdered."

Porter crossed his arms. "What does that have to do with me?"

Cam handed him the handwritten notes. "I was hoping you could make sense of the highlighted part."

Porter's eyes scanned the highlighted bottom of the page then flicked up to the top.

After a solid minute, he said, "I remember a little about this one. Samir Orucov—a real dirt bag. But I couldn't quite nail him down. We had to settle on a lesser charge. I think it was for trying to bribe the officer who brought him in. I did the heavy lifting on the case, but didn't do the arrest."

Cam, who was still standing on the porch, clasped his hands behind his back. "Did you interview the victims of the scam?"

"I believe so." Porter scratched at one of his temples. Shaggy gray hair flopped over his ear. "Are you a P.I. then?"

"I am," Cam said, knowing he didn't have the wherewithal to pass as a police officer to a former cop.

"Stay here," Porter said. He closed the door on Cam. Two minutes later, he reopened it and toddled outside with a blanket around his shoulders and a glass of water in hand. He pointed to a patio set on one side of the porch. Cam pulled out a mesh-backed chair for Porter and sat in another.

Porter clinked the glass onto the table and laid the copy of the handwritten notes beside it. "Orucov the murder victim?"

Cam nodded.

"I'm not surprised."

"Why's that?" Cam asked.

"His sort always end up in the pen or the grave. People don't like being had."

"They never change their ways?"

Porter snorted. "Maybe one in a hundred. You'd have a better shot picking a winner at the track."

Cam leaned in toward the retired officer. "What can you tell me about the mortgage fraud scheme?"

Porter scratched the back of his scalp against the mesh of his chair and relayed a story not unlike the one Kacey had pieced together from the police file.

"How about the victims?" Cam asked when he finished.

"It's hard for me to remember them." Porter sipped his water. "With a rare exception, victims aren't nearly as memorable as the knaves. That's what my chief used to call them—always showing off his vocabulary." His eyes clouded. "Life's a funny duck. Master's from Columbia and he's pounding out security office shifts at Target in retirement. And I'm living off the fat of the land."

"How does that happen?"

Porter's eyes refocused. "He has a pair of ex-wives and six kids. Me, I'm a lifelong bachelor. Same as my uncle—he left me this place."

"Does the name Markuss Vitolins ring a bell?" Cam asked. "Or Piper?"

Porter wrinkled his nose. "Maybe. It's been a long time."

Cam slid his phone out of a jacket pocket and brought up an image of Markuss—a shot surreptitiously snapped when he and Mitzy had discussed the partnership with Markuss and Jana. He turned the phone to face Porter. "I know it's close to thirty years ago, but does this man look like the victim you interviewed with the initials M.V.?"

Porter stared at the picture. He squeezed shut his eyes then looked at the photo again. "Take away the liver spots, add a tuft or two of hair around the ears, and that definitely looks like him."

Cam breathed in deeply. *Meaning Markuss Vitolins had lied to Kacey about living in New Jersey and being conned by Samir.* Cam flicked his finger across the screen. "And could this have been P.V., the child you referred to in your notes?" He twisted a blurry picture of Piper in Porter's direction.

The elder man glanced at it. "Definitely not. One thing I remember for certain. The child was a boy."

***

"A boy," Kacey said.

"Yes," Cam replied with the aid of a hands-free device. He was all of one hour into the trek back to Rusted Bonnet. "Do you have any idea of who that could be?"

"With the first initial 'P'? I don't. But I need to talk to Bernie, pronto. Piper's still locked up and it sounds like good 'ol Markuss didn't tell me the truth. That's obstruction 101."

"Why would he lie?" Cam asked.

"I don't know, but I need to zero in on him. Not only did he fib about being scammed by Samir, but he's been attacked twice, benefitted from Samir's business dealings, and has a Swiss cheese alibi for the time that his partner was killed."

Chapter 23

Cam spent the next nine hours of driving home deep in thought —about his lonesome years in Falls Church, Kacey and Emma, Samir's death, and the attacks on Markuss. The incident with Blair no longer weighed on his mind. He could handle a smattering of dirty looks from righteous villagers. After all, *he* was the victim.

Cam stepped onto his porch at just after eleven. Goldenrod-colored streetlights cut through the black pitch of sky. Scavenging his pockets for his house keys, he sensed a presence to his right.

Cam craned his neck to see Jalil staring up at him from the Adirondack-style bench. The Azerbaijani's eyes glowed saffron disks. Startled, Cam snapped his head back. "Aren't the police looking for you?" he said.

"I believe so. Though I can't imagine why. I only just arrived in the States."

"Where have you been since leaving Mitzy's?"

"Here and there." Jalil stood. "Mind if we go inside for a minute. It's pretty cold out."

A pulse of fear shot through Cam's veins, but he steeled himself. "No problem." He unlocked the door and led Jalil inside.

Cam flicked on the kitchen lights. "I just finished a long drive and could use a beer. Do you care to join me?"

"Sounds good." Jalil rested his hands on the countertop as Cam retrieved bottles of Goose Island and uncapped them. "Your eyes, they do look tired," Jalil commented.

"I've been burning the midnight oil from both ends," Cam said. He handed a beer to the large man and sat on a stool. "Will you be going back to Baku soon?"

"I don't think so. The mafia are no longer gunning for me, but you never know when they'll change their minds."

"I think that's why the police want to talk to you. They want to ask if the mafia could've killed Samir."

Jalil laughed, a throaty noise. "They wouldn't come here. Samir is peanuts, not worth their time. Besides, I paid them in full."

"Why did you owe them money?" Cam asked. He also still hadn't figured out what Jalil was doing in his kitchen.

Jalil flipped his hands in the air. "I made some mistakes. Samir wanted to invest in Azerbaijan. Real estate. So, he pulled money out of his funeral home and I put it into apartment buildings in Zaqatala. The not so nice kind."

According to Mitzy, Jalil said Samir was using the money to bribe government workers in a scam, Cam thought. "How is the mafia tied into real estate?"

"They control everything in the region. You have to pay them an honorarium on every piece of property you buy. Like a tax."

"And what happens if you don't?"

"They damage the building until you pay. Sledgehammers and pickaxes. Not fires—you can't force payment on something that burns to the ground."

"If you made the payments, why were the mafia after you?"

"Like I said, I made some mistakes. I paid them monthly at first, no problems. But then I got greedy." He grimaced. "Samir was sending me money by Western Union each month for the mortgages and mafia's cut. I thought I could double it in the betting pools and keep the winnings for myself. Many of the football matches are fixed and I know lots of people. Easy money. I just never had the capital to take advantage of it." He chugged his beer.

"What happened?"

"I lost. Well, I won a couple of times at first, then I put down a large amount and the game didn't come out how I thought it would. Simple as that. So, I was behind on both the mortgage payments and the honorarium."

Cam took a swallow of beer. His head ached from the drive. "To the tune of a three hundred-thousand-dollar lump sum?"

Jalil touched a finger to his cheek. "You know a great deal."

"Is that why you're here?" Cam ventured. "Looking for information from me?"

Jalil tsked. "I'm here because *I* have information to share with the police, but I don't want to go to the police. Mitzy tells me you used to be married to one of the officers."

"The deputy, yes."

"Good, then I'll tell you and you'll tell her. But it has nothing to do with the three hundred thousand dollars."

"And what if I call her right now and tell her you're here?"

"Then I walk out the door. It's as simple as that." He touched a hand to his hip.

Does he have a gun? "Understood," Cam said nervously.

"The three hundred grand paid off our debts and the whole of the apartment building mortgages," Jalil said.

"So, you didn't try to bribe government workers?"

Jalil groaned. "Mitzy, Mitzy. She's too much. She told you that, correct?"

"Correct."

"That's what she wanted to believe. It's the way Samir used to operate."

Cam waited. After thirty seconds, Jalil closed his eyes and drained the rest of his beer.

"Why pay off the properties in a lump sum?" Cam asked. "What was wrong with the monthly payments? Once you caught up with the amount you lost betting." Cam leaned against the refrigerator.

"Samir was planning to move home." Jalil's voice didn't waiver. "He wanted the apartments to be free and clear when he got there."

"Home? As in Azerbaijan?"

"Yes. Back to Baku." He lifted his empty bottle in Cam's direction.

"Another?" Cam asked and retrieved one for Jalil before he responded. "Was he planning to take Mitzy with him?"

"To be honest, I'm not sure. Probably, but he didn't tell me one way or another." He set the empty on the counter.

Mitzy was moving back to Baku now. Had that been her intent all along—to go with Samir?

Cam blew warm air into a fist. "What do you want me to pass along to the police?" he asked.

Jalil's eyes swept away from Cam's, toward the dining room. "Samir wasn't operating any scams himself. He was selling them. Here in the States, that is."

Cam swallowed hard. "Like a beautiful woman drugging men and making copies of their house keys."

"To sell to a burglar, yes. That's a classic. Easy pickings."

Cam stifled a groan. "And what was Samir's role?"

"He's the professor. He finds a person willing to work the

con and teaches them how to pull it off."

"And he takes a cut of the proceeds?"

"Of course."

"It must be hard to find students. How could he be sure they wouldn't turn him in to the police?"

"You are correct. Samir said that was the hardest part. But he learned to read people. Also, some came to him."

"How's that? Did he have a reputation in some sort of underground circle?"

Jalil shook his head. "Nothing like that." He picked up the Goose Island. "Now, let me tell you about Samir's real gem. It makes a Rohypnol trick look like child's play."

***

Twenty minutes later, Jalil was gone and Cam had a very good suspicion of exactly who had killed Samir. If correct, then he and Kacey had been right about one thing—it was a two-player game, one insider and one person from the outside. Only the outsider was no stranger.

Thursday, February 18

"Do you keep personnel records?" Cam asked. At eight o'clock in the morning, he had pounded on the front door of Paul Bearer's until Mitzy finally responded.

She stood before him with matted hair stinking of stale rum and a bathrobe so loosely cinched that Cam could see the inner curves of her breasts. He averted his eyes.

"You come to me while it is still dark and want what? Records?" Mitzy smacked her lips. "My mouth is dry. I need water. Come in."

He followed her to the break room where she promptly filled

and downed a Big Gulp-sized cup of tap water.

When she finished, Cam said, "I'm looking for accounts of when people were working, when they went on vacation, things like that."

"Samir kept a calendar with those days." Mitzy rubbed her eyes. "Whatever do you want it for?"

"Just trust me."

***

Armed with three years' worth of flimsy "Girls with Guns" calendars, and accompanied by a skeptical Mitzy—who had insisted on showering, blowing out her hair, and applying dollops of cream to her skin before venturing out—Cam's next stop was the Macomb County Medical Examiner's office. With patience that would leave a Department of Motor Vehicles patron in awe and Mitzy's stamp of approval as the deceased's late wife, Cam walked out two hours later with an official copy of Samir's autopsy report, including close-up photos of his body.

***

Despite her protestations, Cam still hadn't clued in Mitzy to the full scope of his ruminations when he dropped her back at Paul Bearer's shortly after noon. He spent another hour waiting, this time for Kacey at the police station, then dropped his haul of papers onto her desk with a thud.

"I need you to look up burglaries statewide corresponding to these dates," Cam said without preamble. He pointed to the top sheet on the stack—a handwritten list of days he had culled from the calendars. "Maybe Ohio and Indiana, too."

"Cam, you can't just walk in here and start making

demands," Kacey said. Seated behind a desk piled with as many empty Styrofoam cups and chewed plastic pen caps as folders, her eyes looked tired—puffy, red, and just plain spent.

"Maybe not, but I know who killed Samir."

Kacey cracked a smile. "You think you did it again?" she whispered.

"I'm positive."

Chapter 24

"Jalil's on a flight back to the near East," Cam said. "Istanbul via Hamburg." After Kacey downloaded two years of Michigan's burglary records, she and Cam had picked up Emma from school together, dropped her off at the only dance studio in the village—for her weekly jazz class—and returned to Kacey's police cruiser, the engine running and heat wheezing through ancient vents.

"You should have told me sooner," Kacey said. "I wanted to talk with him." She cracked a pocket-sized hand warmer and pressed her palms to it. The temperature of the outside air had dipped into the teens.

"Sorry. Of course, I have no idea if he's telling me the truth. He could just as well be in Shane's apartment right now. Or a pay-by-the-week motel somewhere." Cam flipped through the burglary records.

"Are they everything you hoped for?" Kacey asked.

"I think so. You'll want to call the officers who handled each of these. I suspect they'll all have a story in common. In isolation, one that's quite unique."

Kacey pushed out her lower lip. "Now you're just being …
annoying. Emma's class is only an hour long. Spill it."

Cam blew into his hands. "Samir was in the business of
selling cons. To Blair for one." He quickly described the set-up
as Jalil had relayed it, then added, "but that's not the trick that
got him killed. What got him killed was the one he sold to
Markuss and his *wife*." He made air quotes with his fingers.

"Jana?"

Cam nodded. "According to Jalil, she was the real brains
behind the couple. But Jana's not Markuss's wife, she's his
sister."

"His sister?" Kacey shouted.

"Yes, and she has a son named Paul."

"P.V.?"

"Bingo. Apparently, Jana was reckless in her younger years.
Not only was she an unwed mother, which isn't a big deal these
days, but she abused alcohol."

"You'd never know it to see her now."

"That's for sure. She's as buttoned-up as it gets—at least
outwardly. And according to Jalil, who of course got all of this
from Samir, Jana was in a rehab clinic when Samir ran the
check washing scam on Markuss."

"And the son was living with Markuss."

"You're two for two." Cam grinned.

"I can't believe they're not married."

"Believe it."

"I'm missing something," Kacey said after a moment.
"Samir ripped off Markuss in Cape May, then he turns around
and works a con with the man?"

"More like bought a scheme from him."

"That doesn't make sense."

"It does if you're looking for easy money. And Jana was.
After she was rehabilitated and her son grew up and moved on

with his life, she wasn't living well. She had a tiresome job—some sort of menial labor. Her brother had a decent enough life as a bachelor, but embalming isn't like being a doctor. The pay is more like forty or fifty grand a year—middle class, and on the lower end if you live in New Jersey."

Kacey touched the hand warmer to each cheek in turn, then handed it to Cam.

He pressed it against the back of his neck. "So, Jana brainstormed. And she's no dummy. She was smart enough to realize that the best way to do something is to find someone who knows the ropes and learn from him."

"She was impressed with Samir?"

"That's what Jalil said. Markuss fussed constantly about how he'd been conned and that the guy who did it got away with no more than a slap on the wrists. So, much to Markuss's chagrin, she tracked down Samir here in Rusted Bonnet."

"And they moved?"

"Yes. They didn't tell Samir who they were at first, but it's not like Markuss was using an alias."

"Did Samir remember him?"

"His name, yes. They never met in person. Apparently, Samir didn't mind. He would have been more nervous had Markuss been surreptitious. And the timing was just right—the old embalmer was retiring and Markuss had the one credential a small-town funeral home requires."

"A pulse?"

"You got it."

"So, who approached whom about a con?"

"Neither. Jana was the gas in this racecar. Samir had basically retired from illegal enterprises after his stint in Leavenworth. Jana talked him back into the game."

"So, Jana and Markuss came before Blair."

"Jalil didn't know anything about the roofie scam. Well, I

shouldn't say that, he was familiar with it. But he didn't know Samir had taught anyone to run it here in the States."

"How does Jalil know so much about Jana and Markuss?"

"I think he and Samir were close." Cam handed the warmer back to Kacey. "Want to get some drive-through coffee?"

"That sounds good." Kacey jammed the gear shift into reverse and backed out of their spot in the dance studio lot. She pulled onto the street. "So, I think I've waited long enough. What were Markuss and Jana doing?"

Can smiled. "Sorry. It's a burglary con."

"I could've figured that out with the ruby and all." Kacey turned into a fast-food driveway a minute later. "Just coffee?"

"Please. Black."

"I know." Kacey cracked her window and a shot of cold air spat into the car. She shouted an order toward a crackling gray box.

"The ruby was just to throw off the police. It had nothing to do with the con. For each of the past few years, Markuss and Jana have taken three separate weeklong vacations," Cam said. "Every four months or so. Mitzy said she thought they had a timeshare in Tennessee. But according to Jalil, they never went that far."

Kacey pulled her cruiser up to a window and exchanged a wrinkled five for a pair of paper cups with a bespectacled blonde, then turned into a nearby parking spot.

Cam lifted the lid on his cup and blew. The liquid meniscus swelled. "They would target a home in advance and scout it. Jana didn't work so she could do that during the day without raising suspicion while Markuss was at one funeral home or the other. She'd pick out a house in a well-to-do neighborhood and track the family's movements for days on end. If she couldn't discern a pattern, she moved on until she found a place where the residents' movements were regular. Daily pattern was one of the two main criteria. They were also looking for a couple in their forties who had children. It didn't matter how many or how old the kids were as long as they lived at home and, like the parents, left the house during the day. Either at school or day care. No live-in nannies allowed."

Kacey peeled back the seal on a disposable cup of creamer and dribbled the dairy into her coffee. "They didn't give me a stirrer." She pressed down the lid on her cup and swirled gingerly.

"Once they settled on a home, a quick check of the mailbox revealed the adult occupants' names," Cam said. "Armed with a last name, Jana secured fake driver's licenses for herself and Markuss with last names matching the homeowners."

"What if the husband and wife went by different last names?"

"I didn't ask Jalil, but I imagine Jana just chose one—seeing as how they were going to pretend to be the parents of one or the other."

"The parents?"

Cam nodded.

"Where did they get fake IDs?"

"I asked Jalil. He had no doubt Samir would've had a connection he could pass along."

"So, what next?"

"A search of international flights. Delayed flights, actually."

"This is starting to sound complicated." Kacey sipped her coffee. "The heat feels good in my throat."

"Mine, too." Cam took another taste. "It's actually tremendously straightforward, which is what makes it work so well, I imagine. There are websites that show delayed flights into any given airport. So, on the morning of the burglary they were planning, they simply found a flight coming in from Europe that was going to be a few hours late. It didn't even have to be coming directly into Detroit or Cleveland or whichever airport was closest to the target's house—it could be going to JFK or Dulles."

"A connecting hub?"

"Yes. Just as long as the flight could be easily brought up on a smart phone. To show the police."

"Keep going."

"Once they found a flight, Markuss and Jana waited until the family left the home for the day, according to their routine. Then one of them would pick the lock to the front door. A simple enough task for Samir to teach, as long as they didn't care whether they triggered an alarm. And they didn't care. In the class of home they intended to rob, there was always an alarm."

"So Markuss and Jana are in an empty home, alarm bells blaring," Kacey recapped.

"Exactly. Depending on what kind of service the homeowners had, either the alarm company would call the police directly or first put in a call to the home. That was another requirement—that the family have a landline. Landlines may be a dying breed, but there are enough still around and the information is easily obtainable from the white pages. The con would blow up if the alarm company dialed a mobile phone."

"Any time I accidentally trip mine, the company calls and asks for a code number. That's how they confirm you're the homeowner. How would Markuss and Jana get that?"

"They didn't." Cam set his coffee in a center console cup holder. "It was part of their act—to play dumb. If the alarm company called, Jana would pick up the phone and say 'oh dear, I don't know my daughter's passcode,' or something like that. And the alarm company would be obligated to call the cops."

Kacey frowned. "Police, please."

"Sorry."

"So, whether the alarm company called the house first or not, the police were going to show up?"

"Correct. A car usually arrived in five minutes or less."

"That's not a lot of time, especially if they wanted to scour the place for jewelry."

"They didn't rob a thing before the police came. Markuss would pull their car into the garage. Meanwhile, Jana set about to find house keys."

Kacey aimed a quizzical look in his direction but remained silent.

"Often, spares *inside* a house aren't hidden. Usually, there's a set hanging on a hook in the kitchen or mud room. Otherwise, they're in a desk drawer or close to the front door—under the rug or in the foyer closet. If Jana couldn't find a set right away, she kept a set of her own keys on hand for show. By the time the police showed up, Markuss would have made lemonade or iced tea and they'd open the door to the officers, shoes off, drinks in hand, looking at home but gushing apologies."

"A disconcerted set of parents, embarrassed by setting off the alarm at their daughter's house and wasting the police's time."

Cam nodded. "Their daughter and her family were due home from a European vacation. They just drove into town—from several hours away—to take care of their granddaughter because it's her school's winter vacation or spring break or summer something or other." He changed his tone to mimic Jana's voice: "*And see, we have their house keys ... and the last name on our driver's licenses is the same as on their mail ... we're so sorry we forgot the alarm code ... I had it written on a scrap of paper ... I can't believe I left it in my other purse ... would you like some lemonade?*" Then imitating Markuss, "*None of this would have been a problem had their flight not been delayed ... see, it says so right here, three-hour delay— amazing technology phones have these days—Paris to JFK, that's where they're connecting to Detroit from.*" Cam reverted to his normal voice. "Between the pair of befuddled, friendly, apologetic seventy-somethings, the police wouldn't have the chance to get a word in edgewise." "*And we just want to make them dinner so they have a hot meal to come home to after such a long flight. Oh, honey, I left the groceries in the trunk. Our car's in the garage, you see.*" "*And Grammy here is going to set up all the things she needs to play beauty salon with Kimmie so the kids can unpack and then put their feet up.*"

"And the police would let them stay."

"Wouldn't you?"

Kacey took a deep breath. "Probably. That all sounds pretty convincing." She clapped a hand onto the steering wheel. "Then once the police leave, Markuss and Jana rob the place?"

"You guessed it. They can take as long as they need to clean the place out, depending on the schedule of the homeowners. With their car inside the garage, no one sees them loading it, either."

"I wouldn't want to be the officer who let them be after the owners get home and call the blues."

"Deputy egg-on-her-face." Cam smiled. "You'd have to explain that you got conned."

"I bet most of the officers don't. At least not to the home owners. And maybe not even to anyone at the station, unless someone else picked up on the fact that two calls came in from the same house just hours apart. No matter, I'll start by contacting these precincts." Kacey waved the stack of records, which Cam had handed back to her. "I'm hopeful that one or two of the conned officers had the sense to find a sketch artist after they realized what must have happened. Otherwise, all we have is Jalil's word—a jailbird who may be long gone—and the 'coincidence' of Markuss not working on the same days as a handful of burglaries with a similar fact pattern. Knowing the local prosecutors as well as I do, they wouldn't think that's enough for reasonable doubt."

"How about a line-up?" Cam asked.

"That would be step number two—get an officer who met Markuss and Jana to identify them in the flesh. Every little bit helps, but it still might not be enough."

Chapter 25

"I think I've done as much as I can," Cam said.

Bait stared at him blankly. A lack of eyelashes didn't give the poor fish a choice.

"My money's on Markuss and Jana trying to cheat Samir out of his cut of the takings from the burglaries. After all, why pay him? He couldn't very well go to the police. Plus, Markuss knew that Samir sold off Paul Bearer's under Mitzy's nose. Samir wouldn't want her to find out, now would he? So Markuss and Jana stop paying and Samir takes umbrage. No different than the mafia not getting their honorarium on real estate in Zaqatala." Cam gnawed on a celery stalk. "Samir's autopsy photos showed another knife wound—on his thigh. One that was already scabbing. If I had to guess, I bet he and Markuss had an earlier altercation—Samir comes after Markuss in his home and there's a struggle. Samir comes away with a cut on the leg and Markuss is left with blood on the bedroom wall. That's why he was repainting in the dead of winter."

Cam rose and pressed a finger to Bait's tank. The fish finned to the front pane of acrylic.

"I love you, too, buddy," he said. "The two attacks on Markuss were just to throw the police off of his trail. First, Markuss creates a ruse at the movie theater with Shane and uses the time to kill Samir. He and Jana return to the home later that night and she superficially knifes him. Then for good measure, right after Kacey and I question them about the partnership with Samir, they contrive a follow-up attack in their own bathroom. The theft of Mrs. Bitter's ruby is to make the murder look like a robbery gone bad. I suppose they dumped the necklace because they didn't dare pawn it or get caught with it in their possession."

Bait's mouth opened into an "O" shape.

"I know, know, it's all conjecture," Cam said. "Unless Chief Leftwich or Kacey can turn Markuss and Jana against each other, I'm flat out of ideas."

Friday, February 19

"Emma's destined to become the first female director of the FBI," Kacey said.

She and Cam sat atop counter stools at the Bear Claw, waiting on a table—the place was jammed at eight in the morning. Early enough for most of the 9-6ers and just after school buses swept away the attention-demanding population of Rusted Bonnet, junior division.

"Why's that?" Cam sipped coffee. When it came to the morning's first cup, he had no patience for a table.

"She set a trap for Markuss and Jana," Kacey whispered.

"What?" Cam blurted, then choked down the coffee that caught in his throat. "She's seven."

"And already smarter than her mommy." The universal glow of parental pride spread across her face.

Cam admired the eclectic Papier-mâché hot air balloon and

yellow and black prop plane hanging above the breakfast bar. An artist's rendition of a '57 Buick's candy-apple red rear jutted out two feet over the grill.

"She didn't actually set a trap, but inspired me to create one," Kacey said. "Last night at dinner, I was distracted, thinking about the befuddled grandparents con. Over her penne and snap peas, Emma asked me what was wrong. I told her that I had a problem at work—I knew there were some bad people stealing but I couldn't prove it. She asked me why not. I obviously wasn't going to go into the details about the lack of physical evidence or that our source hopped a flight to Istanbul or Damascus or who knows where. So, I just said that no one had actually seen them rob the houses so I couldn't prove it was them."

"Cam, honey, y'alls table's ready." A waitress with a thatch of lemon-yellow hair graying at the roots waved to them.

They wandered to a pistachio green vinyl-backed booth. The waitress refilled Cam's coffee cup, dropped a pair of menus on the veneer tabletop, and scurried away.

"Back to Emma's insight," Cam said.

"Not so much insight as stating the obvious. So obvious that it never crossed my mind. When I told her that no one had caught them in the act, Emma said, 'Why don't you just follow them around until they do it again.'"

"Surely, they wouldn't pull the same scam again now," Cam said and glanced down at a menu he'd studied probably a hundred times. "They might not think the police would tail them, but with Samir dead and Markuss's crummy alibi, I'm sure they'll be laying low. At least for a while."

"I agree." Kacey sipped water. "Unless we offer them something too good to be true."

"A dish best served on a silver platter?"

"Something like that."

"Did Emma lay out a plan?" Cam snickered.

"Don't underestimate your daughter," Kacey lectured. "She said, mommy, it's too bad you don't know what house they want to steal from."

"A set up?"

"Yes, but not one that follows their usual M.O. Bernie and I brainstormed over the phone last night. Markuss and Jana's scheme depends on weeks of watching a family's movements. Plus, how would we bring a family that fit their criteria to them? No, we came up with something more creative. And I need your help."

Cam groaned and, at the same moment, the waitress turned to them. "Menu look that bad today?"

"No, no, Maddie, it's fine. I'll have two eggs over medium and half of a grapefruit."

"Hot sauce for your eggs, right?"

Cam nodded.

"And you, Deputy?"

Kacey patted her stomach twice, "What the heck, farmers scramble with the turkey bacon and dry rye."

"Coffee or juice?"

"I'll stick with water, thanks."

Maddie shuffled away.

"No coffee this morning?" Cam asked.

"I went through an entire pot at home."

"So why do you need me? After Blair and the Galaxes, I'm not sure I'm up for much more."

"Other than sleuthing on your own, Mr. 'I drove to the East Coast.'"

Cam winced. "Okay, why me?"

"Because I need to use Peachy Kleen as a cover."

***

By six-thirty that evening, Cam, Kacey, and Bernie were ensconced in the chief's office. A spiders' web of wires spread across his desk, connecting sundry listening devices—apparently, the wireless age hadn't yet reached Rusted Bonnet police headquarters. For twenty minutes, Becka and Tabby spoke rarely and idly on the other end of the transmission—the local YMCA women's locker room. Swim aerobics class was scheduled to start at seven. Each woman donned a wire taped to her torso, hidden under a towel wrapped around her body. With wet hair and flip flops, they appeared to have just finished a swim.

A far as Cam knew, Becka had expressed very little emotion since the phone call with Dominic Ellum. Malika's concern over her daughter had shifted—from Becka overspending to distress about her slipping into depression. "A mom making up for lost time on the worry-meter," Samantha had suggested, not unkindly. Becka had, however, readily if not eagerly, agreed to Cam's request to help the police.

At six-fifty, the speakers in Bernie's office filled with the sounds of jostling and whispers. *Tabby and Becka had spotted Jana entering the women's locker room to change for aerobics and were moving closer to her as planned,* Cam thought.

A locker creaked. In her South African lilt, Becka said, "Good swim. I'm glad you suggested it."

"When you get to my age, you need it," Tabby replied. "And a nice start to the weekend."

"I wish," Becka said. "I still have that gaudy behemoth in Birmingham to clean. The McMasters's place."

"Are you kidding?" Tabby replied. "That place is gorgeous. Marble as far as the eye can see."

"I suppose, but those statues in the dining room are ridiculous. What I like is the missus's jewelry. I have to admit I've tried on a piece or two just for a spot of fun."

"Don't let Cam hear you say that," Tabby said.

"I'm not worried about him. Cam's a big push over."

From his seat in the chief's office, Cam smiled. The ladies were playing their role well. He hoped Jana was nearby, taking it in.

"You're doing it solo?" Tabby asked.

"Yes. I told Cam I needed the extra money. Problem is, I just remembered that I'm supposed to go with my mother to Kalamazoo tomorrow. There's a hip specialist out there—someone originally from Mombasa. He and his wife invited us to pay them a house call over lunch. It's the East African way."

"Your mom can't go by herself?"

"I think she wants company for the drive. Plus, there's a son."

The sound of Tabby's laugh reverberated. "A fix up."

"We'll see," Becka said. "So, I'm headed to Birmingham tonight. If I start by eight and go straight through, I think I can be done by one o'clock in the morning. Two at the latest. I'll grab a catnap before the drive."

"You can't do that—the owners won't want you cleaning while they sleep."

"They went to San Francisco for the weekend."

"Ah," Tabby said knowingly. "Let me guess. The key's under a flower pot?"

"In one of those stupid plastic rocks!" Becka laughed. "Those don't fool anyone. They don't even have an alarm—too cheap to pay ADT, I guess."

"But I bet they have signs in front of the porch," Tabby said.

"Of course. Stickers on the windowpanes, too. No one would suspect it wasn't armed to a tee."

Saturday, February 20

Birmingham, Michigan had a single White Pages listing for McMasters. And the patriarch of the family happened to be a friend of Bernie's who owed him a favor. So, by six o'clock in the morning, Bernie, Kacey, and police from three neighboring villages spread a net across the home's property, inside and out. As soon as Jana slid into the pool at the Y, Becka had called and confirmed that Jana had, in fact, been within earshot of the entire contrived conversation.

Unbeknownst to Kacey and her colleagues, Cam looked down on the McMasters' mansion through binoculars—George McFly style—from an overhead tree. Emma had been with his mother since school ended the previous day—a standard sleepover at Nana Darby's had turned into a weekend jaunt to an indoor water park and lodge.

Cam knew Kacey's plan wasn't foolproof. She'd concocted an opportunity based on a straight-up burglary rather than one fitting neatly into Markuss and Jana's standard protocol. But Cam was convinced that the Vitolins siblings were sure to snatch it. His biggest worry, as he, Kacey, and the chief had batted around while waiting for Jana to arrive at the Y, was that a defense attorney would slap down an entrapment defense faster than a germaphobe dousing her hands with sanitizer after passing through an Indian buffet. Bernie insisted the argument wouldn't stick because the Vitolins had a propensity for home invasion. Kacey wasn't so sure, but said that even if a burglary charge was tossed during legal proceedings, it was a small price to pay—she was intent on cementing a motive for murder, namely to confirm that Markuss and Jana were thieves who killed Samir to cut out his share of their housebreaking gambit.

Bolts of heat shot through Cam's thighs, his knees pinching either side of a generous branch. His stomach pushed flat against thin bark, Cam arched his neck and back skyward in an ungraceful yogi's cow pose, and peered down at the McMasters' plot.

Seventy-five minutes later, his bladder aching from an ill-conceived morning grind of Dunkin' Donuts-branded beans, a late model Lincoln curled into the McMasters' short driveway. In the light of early dawn, Cam twisted his binoculars into focus. Markuss Vitolins, dressed in jeans and a heavy overcoat, with a Starbucks cup in hand, stomped around to the passenger's side and opened the door for his sister. Bright blue earmuffs matched Jana's parka. Completely conspicuous. Looking like they belonged, should a neighbor be watching. Robbing with panache.

Markuss stepped up the walk, Jana trailing a pace behind, their eyes appearing to scan the ground. Seconds later, Markuss bent toward a patch of stones scattered about the base of a baby Japanese maple bush and rummaged about with what appeared to be latex gloved hands. Without looking back, he stepped onto the porch and popped the lock on the front door. A quick boot stomp on the mat and the couple entered the grand home, quietly shutting the window into Cam's personal peep show.

Five minutes later, the pair reemerged flanked by uniformed officers, hands cuffed behind their backs. Jana shouted, "You're mistaken. Our daughter lives here!" Markuss's face appeared as an ashen mask. Moments later, a sea of flashing lights flooded the street—three police cars nosed-in behind the Town Car, a vehicular peace sign sans circle from Cam's vantage point. Kacey emerged from the center cruiser and spoke briefly with one of the Vitolins' escorts. She barked into a mobile phone, then corralled Markuss and Jana into the back seat of her cruiser.

Chapter 26

There's nothing like a big family dinner. Not of the Sunday's best variety, but a Saturday night special, replete with three generations of Reddicks. A fire crackled in Cam's living room. Darby tried to teach Emma the cha-cha, but the girl insisted on showing her grandmother moves gleaned from countless episodes of *American Ninja Warrior*.

In the kitchen, Cam sipped a Trader Joe's pinot noir, using his free hand to intermittently swap between stirring lamb ragout with one wooden spoon and butternut squash soup with another. Kacey swirled the dregs of her chardonnay. "You need an apron," she said.

"Kiss the cook?" Cam teased. "Sorry."

"I'm not touching that!" Kacey laughed. "Thanks for hosting. I can't believe it's over."

"I saw you bring in Markuss and Jana this morning," Cam said.

"You were downtown when I booked them? I didn't see you."

Cam looked down at the bubbling orange soup. "I didn't

want to get in the way," he said, avoiding any mention of his lurking in the tree. "Did you just charge them with attempted burglary or did the chief let you hit them with murder, too?" He looked up at his ex-wife. Her lips stretched into a broad smile.

"It was only breaking and entering until about noon." She blushed. "Then I flipped Jana."

"Really?" Cam felt a surge of pride. "That's amazing!" He set his glass on the counter and wrapped Kacey into a hug.

"What's happening in there?" Darby asked from the other room.

"I'll tell you later," Kacey said loudly. "All good news."

"Nana, can we have a Selena Gomez dance party?" Cam heard Emma ask. Thirty seconds later, the latest pre-teen track launched.

"How did you get Jana to turn on her brother?" Cam asked Kacey.

"For leniency on the B&E charge."

"What did she say?"

"She admitted that she helped in the cover up, but that Markuss wielded the knife. She claimed that she didn't know anything about it ahead of time. She said he took her to water aerobics after work, then used Shane as a dummy to establish an alibi and kill Samir."

"Did she tell you why?"

"Markuss was tired of paying Samir twenty-five percent of the take from the burglary scam."

"That's what I figured."

"She claimed that she didn't know anything about a fight in the bedroom of their house, and had no idea that Markuss was painting to cover up blood."

"How could she not know?"

"Well, they are siblings, not spouses. She said the master bedroom was Markuss's. She slept in the guest room in the basement."

"So, she didn't know he was going to off Samir?"

"That's her story. Not that I necessarily believe her."

"I don't even know if I believe that Markuss is the killer. The angle of the knife suggested a woman did it, right?"

"The upward angle was consistent with a person shorter than Samir stabbing him. But, Markuss has arthritis in his shoulder. Jana said he stabbed Samir *underhanded*."

Cam ground cracked pepper into the soup pot. "I can't believe I didn't think of that."

"Jana claimed that after he came home, Markuss begged her to go back to Paul Bearer's and cut him."

"Him, Markuss?"

"Yes. To throw off suspicion. She said he bit on a cloth, so Mitzy wouldn't hear him if he screamed in pain. Of course, she was probably too passed out to hear anything."

"Then Jana took the cloth and knife with her?"

"That's what she said."

"Hold on." Cam held up a wooden spoon. Orangish-brown drops of butternut puree rained down onto the cooktop. "The knife you found in the snow with Markuss's dried blood was taken from Piper's kitchen. How did they manage that?"

"Same story from Jana."

"That it was all Markuss?" Cam swept a paper towel across the soup drops. He cursed at the smear.

"It's what she claims. He stole Piper's knife ahead of time."

"This all seems awfully one-sided." Cam wet a dish cloth with water and cleaned the soup smudge properly.

"I agree. She seems to be more cunning than he is. *But*, her testimony will completely sink Markuss."

"And what about Jana? Did Markuss turn on her?"

"Not yet. Of course, we have them separated. We told Markuss that his sister made him the lone bad guy, but he doesn't believe us. He will soon enough, I expect."

"I almost feel bad," Cam said. "Even though Samir was puppeteering cons, tied to the Azerbaijani mafia, and sold Paul Bearer's out from under Mitzy's nose, it seems that everyone in his life was better off with him alive. Markuss and Jana had a cushy gig and are now going to prison, Mitzy's headed back to Baku with almost nothing to her name, and Piper's jobless after years of steady work. The same goes for Shane and Jelly Roll. And Blair's gig is up, not that her downfall stemmed from Samir's murder."

"But think of all of the people Markuss, Jana, and even Blair hurt. Plus, Mitzy doesn't get much sympathy from me." Kacey smiled. "And not just because she tried to get you into bed."

Cam reddened. "I guess Shane and Jelly have been living off the fat of the land for a long time, too."

"Piper's the only one who I feel for. But she knows the trade well—I'm sure she'll land on her feet soon enough." Kacey plucked the wooden spoon from the soup pot and touched her tongue to it. "This is delicious."

"Thanks," Cam said and ladled ragout into a serving bowl. "I learned everything I know from the Barefoot Contestant."

Kacey laughed. "A week or so from now, de Winter's bringing the cranes back in. Strip mall city."

"Caskets to Go?"

"Why not. Wedged between a Chinese buffet and a dollar store."

"Dinner's ready, ladies!" Cam shouted to his mother and daughter. He carried the lamb ragout to the dining room table, Kacey trailing with the soup. Emma raced in and sprang onto her seat, followed by her grandmother gracefully sliding into hers—a foursome settling down to a perfect winter night's supper.

About the Author

Corpse & Robbers is the second installment of Stephen Kaminski's Male Housekeeper Mystery series.

Kaminski also pens the Damon Lassard Dabbling Detective Mysteries.

He is the recipient of the Murder & Mayhem Award for Best Classic Cozy, multiple Reader Views Literary Awards, and was a Chanticleer Media CLUE Award finalist.

Other Titles by Stephen Kaminski:

Male Housekeeper Mysteries
An Au Pair to Remember (Cozy Cat Press, 2019)

Damon Lassard Dabbling Detective Mysteries
Murder, She Floats (Cozy Cat Press, 2014)
Don't Cry Over Killed Milk (Cozy Cat Press, 2013)
It Takes Two to Strangle (Cozy Cat Press, 2012)